THIS DARK ARCHITECT

AND OTHER GRIM TALES

PAMELA JEFFS

For Wayne

PRAISE FOR PAMELA JEFFS

In *This Dark Architect and Other Grim Tales*, Jeffs takes us into worlds of darkness and decay in which the slow tread of the survivor is like the beat of a bitter heart. Stories of sadness and sacrifice, in which hope glitters like a black diamond, and reminds us that love makes us hold tight, even sometimes when we should let go. This is a masterclass of insightful story telling.

— MATT TIGHE, AUREALIS AND AUSTRALASIAN SHADOWS AWARD WINNING AUTHOR.

Pamela's writing is like a powerful picture painted with brilliantly coloured words. It pins the reader from the first sentence and to the last word, leaving you craving more.

— MARIA WILLIAMS, AUTHOR OF 'A GIRL OF NO IMPORTANCE AND OTHER POEMS'.

CONTENTS

Death Interrupted   9
Stokehold   36
Of Slaves and Lions   51
Keep the Stitches Small   60
Bones to Feed Fallow Fields   73
New World Order   84
A Mother's Son   105
Tenebrous   115
Desert Gods   136
This Dark Architect   147

Acknowledgments   185
References   187
About the Author   189

DEATH INTERRUPTED

The corrugated, red dirt road snakes away, headed for the North Queensland horizon. The sun beats hot against the back of my neck, a prickling heat that, when paired with the humidity, shouts 'tropical climate'. It's taken three months walking through a post-apocalyptic New South Wales to get here, traversing landscapes littered with the corpses of those who stood up against the brain-mad, full-mech government. Those who refused to be taken away and 'fixed'.

Most people don't want to live forever. Technology allows us to replace our fragile organs and attain immortality, but we can't replicate the complexities of a human brain. I've seen it happen before, when a person's mind breaks from the weight of living.

I glance at my wrist tracker. Ten kilometres until I reach what I hope will be my final destination. The hidden, re-purposed compound I'm searching for is a tantalising myth claiming to be a haven to bionics like myself—a place where I can retain what remains of my human body.

I'm so close now. The rural routes offer less danger of discovery by the full-mech soldiers that hunt me. It pays to stay alert. Threat lurks in the wreckage that litters even these remote landscapes.

A crumpled, rusted Landcruiser sits against a dirt pile on the side of the road; its split rear doors hanging open like a mouth. I imagine the *tick, tick* cadence of a metal heart sitting on an empty seat, still beating for the human half of a body long rotted away.

Nothing stops the bio-organs functioning, even when they aren't needed anymore.

"Hey there! Help!"

I snap my rifle to my shoulder, finger pressed to the trigger. It's been weeks since I've heard another voice, and the last was not friendly.

"Please!"

It's coming from the Landcruiser. Someone's alive inside. Damn. My head says ignore it but my heart…

I approach the rear of the car, palms sweating.

The scent of diesel hits me. A lone broken fuel can sits discarded near the back wheel.

"Please..."

I lower my rifle. An injured woman rests just inside the tailgate, half reclined against the door pillar. She's maybe sixty and all-the-way, old-school human. Made as she was born.

Rare these days, and no threat at all to someone like me.

She tries to sit up but falls back, moaning. Her left leg is injured, the wound clotted and black. Her veiny fingers grip a handgun, but I sense she has little strength or will to aim it.

"Thank God," she says.

I almost laugh out loud. God and my contemptuous self haven't seen eye to eye for many years. He took both my wife and son, saw them slaughtered in the final days of the mech war, hours after I embraced machine-wrought immortality to ensure I could protect them. All God ever taught me was that even a metal heart can shatter with grief.

Now, old hatred, silver prosthetic eyes, and twenty-year-old scars earned from organ and bone replacements brand me as one firmly outside the Lord's dominion.

But the old lady doesn't seem to care.

"You got anything to drink?" she asks. "I've been here two days."

I sling the rifle, unhitch my water bottle, and approach her. My medi-data stream, information that scrolls endlessly to the left of my optic viewscreens, detects damaged flesh.

Calf injury. Cleanse and suture. Administer antibiotics for treatment of imminent infection.

I sigh. My medkit's been empty for weeks.

"What's your name?"

"Petra."

"Here." I hand her the water.

Petra sips slowly. Only someone schooled in survival would know not to gulp it.

"What happened?" I ask.

"I swerved to miss a kangaroo," she says, voice weak. "I crashed and hurt my leg. Couldn't dig the car out and it's too far to walk home."

"I thought kangaroos were extinct."

"Why do you think I swerved?"

"Did it survive?"

"Yeah, but it's cost me." She gestures towards her leg. "Doesn't look too good, does it?"

I shrug. "My scanners say with treatment, you should live."

Petra grimaces. "Any chance you've got medical supplies on you?"

"No. Sorry."

"I guess your kind don't really need them."

"Rarely."

A weak smile curves her lips. "Well, I've got plenty of supplies at the house. Will you help me? I can't get back alone."

I glance up the road. I don't want to deviate from my course.

"You don't look like the abandoning-old-women type," says Petra.

"You know nothing about me."

"You've got kind eyes."

Funny. I can't even remember what my real eyes looked like.

Petra takes a deep breath and the sweat beaded on her brow shimmers. An ominous sign.

"You know my name. What do I call you?" she asks.

"Colton."

She takes another sip and leans back. "Well, Colton, if you don't want to help, that's okay. At least sit with me for a bit. I don't want to die out here alone."

The old lady knows how to deliver a grade-A guilt trip. I frown. This delay irritates. Do I really need to help her?

"You got a shovel?" I ask, giving in.

"You going to dig me a grave?"

"No. I'm going to dig the car out of the mound you drove it into."

It takes me an hour across midday to clear the car from the bank. All I can taste now is iron-rich dust in the back of my throat. I spit to clear it. I swear my saliva sizzles as it hits the road.

The driver's seat groans wearily as I slide into it and turn the engine key. The car stutters and dies. I clench my jaw, pump the accelerator, and try again. This time a thick cloud of black smoke billows out of the exhaust pipe, the motor kicks into life, and an ominous rattle fills the cabin.

"That's normal," says Petra from the rear. "She's an old girl like me. A bit of noise in the knees."

I shake my head, charmed by the woman's sense of humour.

"Where do we need to go?"

"About twenty kilometres north, then take the second turn to the right."

"What were you doing out here?"

Petra shrugs. "Fuel run. There's an abandoned farm I know with an underground storage tank that still has petrol in it."

I nod. Can't fault her for trying to survive.

I reverse from the verge and back onto the road. Fingers crossed this hunk of junk will get us where we need to go.

At least the air conditioning still works. I relish the cold blast of air as the car rumbles down the highway, seat springs squeaking with every corrugation we hit. I've forgotten what it's like to travel in a vehicle, the feel of a turbo diesel engine under me.

Scenery flashes past the window. My mind drifts in the watercolour blur of dusky green vegetation, sapphire skies, and vibrant red earth.

"Turn's coming up here," Petra yells over the sound of the motor.

I return to myself with a jolt, slamming the brakes on hard and almost missing the track. A cloud of dust billows past.

"Watch it!" Petra snaps.

"Sorry."

The path is nothing more than a faint trail leading away into the bush. A secret entrance of sorts. The old lady is smart. I guess she'd have to be, though, to survive where most haven't.

I take it gently, easing over the bumps to limit

Petra's discomfort. We circle around grass trees and the great monolithic termite mounds that tower between the stringybarks.

"Stop by the next pile of boulders," says Petra. "You'll need to get out to deactivate the gate sensor."

"What gate?"

"You'll see."

My visual scanners beep in warning. Between the rocks is the faint heat signature of concealed explosives.

"It's rigged?"

"Security," she says. "I've had problems in the past. Control panel is at the base under the smallest rock. Code is eight-three-eight-four-two-four."

I ease the car to a halt. The door opens with a screech, letting the outside rush in. The air smells different to the sun-baked earth of the highway; here it's heavy with the scent of sun-warmed eucalyptus. I leap out of the car and deactivate the trigger. Overhead a crow caws. I glance up at the raven bird, its blue-black feathers gleaming and its pale eye fixed to mine. A sense of foreboding washes over me. I frown and push it away. I don't believe in omens.

Once past the gate, we proceed on. The vegetation soon crowds closer to the road, narrowing to a driveway. Two hundred metres further, we exit the trees.

The view past them is unexpected. I take in the lay of Petra's farm as it sprawls below, held in the basin of a hidden valley. Bordered on all sides by virgin forest, it's like a long-lost photograph of how the world used to be.

Rambling gardens frame a sprawling farmhouse and machinery shed. Cultivated fields, sown with a range of vegetables, hug the low-lying areas where the soil is black and fertile. A dark river tracks along the valley floor, banks peppered with tea trees and water lilies. Farther off in the distance, a small herd of cattle graze at late wet season grasses.

Yet even here, technology has infiltrated. The fields are worked by androids. Older models from the look of their bulky forms, ten years at least.

And I don't fail to note the additional explosives concealed along the fence lines.

"Park down by the veranda," says Petra. "Then you can help me inside."

It's cool within the house. The rooms smell like warm timber and beeswax. I help Petra to the old but well-maintained leather sofa in her lounge room. She points to an archway beside an ancient grand piano.

"Bathroom is through there. Supplies are in the cabinet."

Beyond the arch stretches a long corridor, its walls heavy with photographs. Some show Petra in her youth, bright-eyed with strawberry blonde hair. In other pictures, she stands proudly next to a hawk-nosed man, her arms cradling a baby. In the last photo on the wall, the child has grown into a tall, handsome youth dressed in a graduation gown.

Grief washes over me. My boy never went to school.

I wonder where Petra's son is now.

The bathroom cabinet is well stocked. I take a handful of bandages, needles, and suturing thread. Betadine to clean the wound. Stacked boxes of medications line the bottom shelf—an impressive stash. I can only guess at where it all came from. I scan the labels and select a course of Cephalexin. No anaesthetic to be seen. Petra will have to brave the stitching on her own.

A glass sits empty on the bench. I fill it from the sink, balancing it in the crook of my elbow. On my way back, I collect a walking cane from the corner of the room.

Petra takes the water and cane with thanks. I lay the rest of the items on the coffee table.

"Found everything?" she asks, holding the glass close.

"Yeah, but there's no local. You okay with that?"

Petra's smile turns grim. "I've run a farm for fifty years. A little pain won't kill me."

I work fast. Petra grits her teeth but stays silent. Soon her leg is cleaned and bound. I retreat and sit on the edge of the piano stool.

Silence fills the room as I think up polite ways to take my leave.

"So, tell me about yourself, Colton," says Petra, her hands shaking as she rests back against a pillow. "Why are you travelling alone out here?"

I purse my lips. How much do I tell her?

"I'm trying to get clear of the cities."

Petra's gaze holds mine. I consider her human eyes. I've never seen blue ones before. These days everyone has optical implants.

"Not much chance of new enhancements out here."

"I'm not concerned. I'd rather stay as human as I can manage."

The old woman moves her leg and winces. "You're headed for the bionic colony, then?"

Shocked, I suck in a breath. The colony was a mere whisper of an idea in the cities; a death sentence if the full-mech soldiers found you believing in it. For that is the madness of their kind—abhorrence of free will and for anyone still holding to the human code of decency.

"You know where it is?"

"I do," she says, "but they aren't too friendly toward strangers. It's dangerous heading there."

I shrug. "Better than the alternative."

Petra frowns. "That bad, huh? I don't get much in the way of news out here."

I've held my secrets close for so long, it sometimes feels as if I'm drowning. Maybe it's time to share. It's been forever since I confided in anyone.

I rub my stubbled chin. "Full-mechs run the national government now and entire body replacements are mandated. You don't get a choice. I needed to get out before I was herded up with the rest of the bionics and modified."

"So much for democracy. I didn't realise."

"They say for humanity to survive, we need to cut out the weakness."

Petra looks away. "There's nothing weak in being human," she says. "Fearing death is our weakness."

I think back on the decisions I've made for myself and realise she's right.

"Colton," says Petra, "you're welcome to stay here for the night. My husband died a few years back and I'd welcome the company." She sounds sad.

"Tomorrow I'll show you the colony's mapped location."

One part of me wants to be on my way, but the other relishes the thought of a night in a comfortable bed. I glance at the window. Outside, the sun is already dipping toward afternoon, leaving the shadows long across the valley.

"Thank you," I say, dismissing my impatience.

Petra's fingers worry at a loose thread on the seat's cushion.

"Unless," she says, "would you consider staying here? You've proven trustworthy and you'd be safe, hidden from the world. I'd be happy to let you call this place home."

The hairs rise on the back of my neck, my sixth sense recognising an indefinable shift in Petra's tone. Desperation, perhaps?

I hesitate, reluctant to offend. "The offer is generous, but I must keep going."

Her hopeful gaze falls into disappointment. "I understand. But please, at least stay for tonight."

"Just for tonight," I say, "but no longer. I need to find my own kind."

Petra sleeps on the couch, chin resting on her chest, her breaths slow and steady. I sit opposite her, watching the sunset fade outside. Even though I'll be leaving tomorrow, the nostalgic serenity of this place appeals to me—the sounds of the house creaking and settling, the gentle low of cattle in the distance, and the unashamedly human company.

My audio sensors register a new sound. An alarm, faint but insistent. I glance at Petra. She's still out of it, getting the rest she needs to heal. Curious, I rise, heading along the corridor towards the soft beeping.

At this late hour, the house is subdued, lit softly by wall lamps in each of the spaces. The day's warmth lingers close, uncomfortable after the weeks spent living out in the open. I stalk past the bathroom, the door still ajar. The alarm rings out again, tinny and small, from deep in the house. Past three closed doors, perhaps leading to bedrooms, I then find the kitchen. Its polished timber floors gleam below dark stone benches. Colour schemes from another time.

The walk-in pantry is open. I ease closer. The sound grows louder and I take a look inside. The room is empty, shelves removed to access a single, metal door at the rear. To the right, a high-tech keypad blinks red in time with the alarm. The words 'low power' flash across a small screen adjacent. The set up is familiar to me, a security lock—one that only opens from the outside.

Something is sealed behind this door…

I press a fingertip to the panel and jump back as the door cracks open with a hiss. It swings away of its own accord, leaving a glaring rectangle of darkness.

"Don't go in. Not yet anyway."

I swivel. Petra stands behind me, propped on the cane. Her pale gaze holds mine.

"What's down there?" I ask.

She takes a deep breath, hobbles to a stool, and sits. "I once had a son."

"I saw your photos."

"He drowned in the river."

I glance at the door. What is she saying? She keeps a locked mausoleum in her kitchen? I bite my lip.

"I couldn't let him go," she continues, "and my husband couldn't bear to see me heartbroken."

A horrific notion forms in my mind and my blood runs cold. "What are you saying?"

"I'm getting old, Colton. Sitting on the side of that road waiting to die made me see the truth of things."

"What are you saying?" I repeat, slower this time to hide my growing sense of unease.

"I'm sorry. Really, I am." Petra's palm opens to reveal a small device. My medi-data stream registers a building electromagnetic pulse. The word 'WARNING' lights up in scarlet letters across my vision.

"No!" I step forward, hand outstretched.

The pulse engages.

My mechanical heart stutters to a stop.

Electricity crackles. Bio-organs buck in response. I lurch upright to the clanking of chains. My wrists are both shackled to the bed rails of a surgical table.

Groggy and stiff-limbed, I draw a breath. The room is unfamiliar—windowless concrete walls, ceiling, and floor. A single cold, electric, white-blue light scowls overhead.

"You weren't out for long. There won't be any brain damage," says Petra.

"Thanks for that," I mutter, sneering.

She stands just out of arm's reach. An android flanks her, an organ-reset booster in its grip.

I glare at the automaton. All chrome exoskeleton and zero humanity. It must have carried and manacled me here.

"What is this?" I growl.

Petra's face twists, a look one part anguish and three parts desperation. "What any mother would do in my position. I need your help."

I jerk the chain on my left wrist. "Why kidnap me? You could've tried asking."

"I did try. You wanted to leave."

My stomach tightens. "Let me go."

Petra shakes her head. "I can't do that. My husband was an engineer, you see. He saved our son's life."

"But you said your son died."

"Yes. We assembled a new body for him."

"What? But his brain wouldn't have been viable for transplant."

"We salvaged what we could."

Sickness curdles my gut. I understand the desperate desire a parent feels to save a child. Once, I considered this same solution to my own grief, but even despairing, I knew not to cross that line. A dead brain put into a full-mech body and reanimated? It breaks the single law on this planet that even the craziest of us respect.

Once they're gone, you don't bring them back.

Petra leans against the bench, easing her weight onto her good leg. She tips her chin to the android. "Open it up, R6."

R6, its movements precise and measured, turns to a control panel. It taps the top three buttons. The rear wall of the room retracts to reveal a pristine white chamber, its entrance barred. Within sits a full-mech man on a low seat, metal skin casings and chrome rivets all polished and gleaming. His green, backlit eyes lift. His fingers twitch.

"This is Grey," says Petra. She smiles at the mech who looks nothing like the boy in the photos. "Say hello to Colton, Grey."

The mech's top lip ripples back. His copper teeth gleam behind a smile that holds no welcome at all.

"Hello, Colton."

I shiver. His tone holds the deep, smooth cadence of a man's, but there's nothing human behind that voice.

"See? The transfer was a success," says Petra, almost pleading. "But that is only the first step. He needs to learn how to fit into society but I can't teach him. I've been gone too long from that world. You know how things work out there. You could show him."

I want to scream at her, tell her how crazy the idea is, but I'm in no position to agitate the situation. I try logic.

"Even if I could help, he's illegal tech, Petra. They'll dismantle him on sight."

"Then stay here and be a father to him."

My heart skips a beat as I recall my own son—his deep brown eyes and soft skin. The way his corpse looked lying next to his mother's.

I've no desire for another child.

I try a different direction. "Why cage him? If he is well, let him try his own path."

Petra's eyes drop, but in the instant before, an emotion shadows them. Shame? Fear?

"He's in there for his own good," she says. "He went for some time without oxygen to his brain. When he awoke, he had amnesia. He can be dangerous. Fear makes him lash out."

It's not amnesia. It's death interrupted.

The thought shatters my patience.

"You know that isn't your son, don't you?" I whisper.

Petra's mouth resolves into a hard, thin line. "He's my *only* son, and I'll do anything to protect him."

I know I've lost the argument. The old woman is as mad as any full-mech who's lived too long.

"Sit with him a while," says Petra, straightening. "You'll realise what I'm asking for is reasonable."

She turns away and R6 follows her out of the room.

The door closes behind them.

Grey's eyes never leave me. He sits unnervingly still on the seat.

I wrestle the chains without luck. "Damn it!" Banging both hands on the edge of the bed, I glance at Grey.

Would he release me if I played nice?

"How long have you been here?" I ask.

The mechanical son lifts his chin. Light glints off his cheek. "I was activated fourteen thousand, six hundred days ago."

It takes me a moment to calculate. *Forty years...*

"Why does she keep you here like this?"

"I killed my father."

My mouth goes dry. So not just dangerous—Grey is a murderer.

Shit.

"Why?"

Grey taps his forehead with one long, elegant, silver finger. "I wanted his memories."

His lips widen to a grin, spontaneous and unnatural. Predatory, even.

My shoulders clench tight with sudden apprehension. "How would killing him give you his memories?"

"Brains are like computers. Information can be downloaded if you know how."

Something warns against me asking him *exactly* how.

Grey tilts his chin, his composure cool as a corpse. "The only thing I recall from my previous life is the act of dying," he says. "That singular event is branded on my mind—the persistent nightmare of darkness, crushing depths, and water clawing its way into lungs I no longer own. I've tried to forget, but no new memory I make ever erases the sensations. I discovered only in taking memories from the living do I find temporary surcease."

Grey falls silent. I sense his particular form of madness is not the same as that of those who want me dead. It's not a life lived too long that drives his desires, but something else—a hunger for life's experiences, I suspect, his own still hidden beyond the veil of death.

Grey offers nothing further. He sits motionless in his all but empty room, dead-eyed and undeniably inhuman. His stillness terrifies me, like he is absent in the moments between words. But I'm not fooled. There's animal cunning at work there. He doesn't need to move. He's already died once and has risen from it. Made immortal, he has nothing left to fear. He has all the time in the world to sit and wait.

I'm tempted to ask more about his origins—at least when he talks, his intelligence lets me pretend he is a normal man—but I fear the answers I'll get. What more do I need to know anyway? He's a killer. His mother fears him enough to keep him caged. If I stay here and watch over him like she has asked, it will be as a guard. And if he ever gets free, I'm afraid he'll kill me too.

I force myself to calm down. Anxiety and inaction here will spell my end. I have to escape from this animated-dead mech and his crazy mother.

But how?

My mind races.

Just out of sight, the pantry door opens again, followed by the thud of a hesitant footstep. Petra appears, leaning on her cane. Her android follows close behind, holding a platter of sandwiches.

"I'm going to release one of your hands so you can eat," she says, nodding to her helper.

R6 approaches and the chains are loosened. Starving, I snatch a sandwich.

"So what's your decision?" asks Petra. "Will you stay on?"

I chew carefully, holding my silence and

wondering what the consequence of saying no would be.

"Have you spoken with Grey?" she asks.

"Yes." I grab another sandwich. "He told me he murdered his father."

Petra shakes her head. "Grey plays games. He makes up memories to fill the space left by those of his own that are missing."

"Hell of a story to make up."

"He isn't dangerous."

I risk a look at Grey. He's listening, proven by the sly smile curling that cold mouth of his. It's creepy enough to consolidate my decision.

"I'll stay."

The lie comes easily. Petra's eyebrows furrow over her slim nose. I wonder if I've made it sound too easy.

"Just to be clear. If I release you and you leave, I'll send every one of my androids to hunt you down and then you'll be tied to this table until your flesh parts rot away."

"You have my word."

"R6."

The android releases my other hand. The chain falls away and I rub my wrist. I slowly curl my hand into a fist and then, with all my strength, punch R6 in the chest panel. The skin across my knuckles splits but the enhanced bones beneath don't buckle. R6's chestplate cracks like an eggshell and the sensitive chips beneath crush like foil. The android's head twitches as its program glitches, then it rallies. It grabs me by the shirt and flings me across the room. I crash against the bars of Grey's cage, grunting as pain shoots across my back and hip. R6 leaps, reaching me in two bounds. It lifts me clear off the floor by my throat.

"Restrain him," screeches Petra.

I dig at the android's hand but it's too strong.

A sudden spray of sparks and the whine of distressed metal jolt me sideways as the android releases its grip. Grey's chrome hand extends through the bars, grabbing R6's cranium and ripping the android's head from its neck socket.

I slither to the floor. Headless, R6 stumbles backwards, crashing into the door's control panel. Its whole body jerks as the open neck wires touch and short-circuit the locking system.

The door to Grey's room clicks open.

Petra, pale as a sheet, flees as fast as she can manage. I hear her cane clicking across the kitchen floor, her sobs at every step.

Grey moves to stand above me. He extends his arm, dropping the android's head into my lap.

"I never liked R6," he says.

Adrenaline has me trembling but I keep my voice calm. "Can't say I was a fan either."

Grey looks at me, features unreadable. "I could kill you too, you know?"

I swallow, my mouth dry as a desert. "Will you?"

"Not yet. I have more pressing work." He glances at the door. "You won't like what comes next but it must happen. I have so many questions and my mother has the answers."

Outside in the kitchen, Petra is screeching on the comms, ordering the farm androids to return to the house.

"What are you going to do?" I ask, again fearing the answer.

His illuminated eyes dim to embers and I try to imagine him as the boy in the pictures—the boy Petra loved enough to break the laws of nature for.

I can't see him.

"I'm a dead thing—a conflicted memory preserved in a machine," whispers Grey, his voice hollow and black. "My 'mother' out there is a face known to me only through my father's recollections. I need to understand why she brought me back. I deserve the peace that comes from knowing."

"How will you get that?"

"By taking her memories too."

Fear-sweat trickles down my back. "Then what?"

Grey pauses, his stillness uncanny.

"Then I'll find other memories to fill the gaps," he says. "I'll feed on other minds."

His threat delivered, Grey stalks past me. He disappears around the corner and Petra's voice, tremulous, filters back from the kitchen. The farm androids haven't made it in time to help her.

"Please, Grey," she whimpers. "Don't do it."

"You should have let me rest in peace."

I wait until Petra's screams stop. The heavy silence that follows crowds in—emptiness filled with shame. I let Petra die. I sat here and listened as he murdered her.

Something heavy is dragged past the pantry door. I taste bitter terror on my tongue.

But then cold resolve fortifies me. Past the fear and dishonour, I am nothing if not a survivor. I've fought too hard to get this far. I refuse to die here like this.

I gather myself up and ease cautiously toward the exit, each bruised muscle protesting the movement. The door stands ajar. I peer around it into the well-lit kitchen.

The metallic smell of blood hangs in the air, and

there's a long sweep of red painted on the floor. I follow the line of gore to the space in front of the fridge.

There, Grey crouches. Poised like a spider, he turns, backlit eyes luminous. Petra's corpse lies at his feet, skull cracked open, oozing blood, black-red, onto the linoleum.

My gorge rises. Grey's chin is slicked scarlet and brain matter fills his fist.

He chews slowly. Thoughtfully.

"In the absence of choice, peace is euphoric, Colton," he whispers, voice distant as he stares into space, attention drawn to whatever visions his mother's mind held.

Not daring to linger, I slowly back out of the room.

There's a highway and freedom out there waiting for me.

STOKEHOLD

Fear had a way of leeching into metal and stone and wood, of creating an invisible patina. In a place where the past was brutal, the dread felt old and dangerous, but in the belly of a battleship, the horror was compounded. Here, in the stokehold, weighted down in furnace light and coal dust, old regrets and torment abounded. Sailors had died here. Some by fire, others by a murderous knife thrust between the ribs at midnight. And the ghosts of those men never left.

Tonight, they seemed restless; their forms, shadowy half suggestions, huddled and shifted in the darker corners of the hold. Not sure what had them riled, but having abided amongst them all my life, I knew I was safe from their words and their touch as long as I kept to the firelight.

I kicked open the furnace door, squinted against the blasting heat, and shovelled another pile of coal onto the grate. Embers rained to the deck as the blaze rose to heat the water in the giant boilers above. Steam hissed in response, fuelling the clock-work mechanisms that propelled the ship.

"Gypsy Boy."

I hunched my shoulders. Why did I ever ask that son of a bitch Zeke if he could see the ghosts too? "I'm here, Chief."

Zeke, senior in rank to me, stalked in from the airlock, his body swaying to counter the motion of the ship. He was big and brawny—coarse, as if cut from rusted steel—and he wore coal dust like armour pressed into the creases of his forty-some-thing-year-old face.

"Captain wants you." He grabbed a shovel from the rack. "Get up there and get back quick. Don't think I'm happy about doin' your work for you."

The captain? I glanced at the ghosts. Their heads were bent together in some kind of silent communi-cation. I didn't want to leave my post. "What do you think he wants?"

"Do I look like I'm fuckin' privy to the desires of officers? Now get yourself goin.'" He shoved past me, dropping his meaty shoulder to my chest and making me stumble. He took my place at the grate and scooped in another load of coal. Patches of sweat stained his shirt, looking blood-dark in the fickle light.

I dropped my shovel and headed for the bridge.

The ghosts with their jittery, smudgy forms trailed single file behind me as I exited into the close crew corridor. They kept their distance for the moment. But, damn, I hated the way they moved— all uncanny-like—the sharp, aggressive blinking in and out of view, the three or four of their steps lost between.

I hated how their eyes and mouths looked like deep, black holes.

Sweat slid down my back and not from the heat. The electric lanterns lining the walls here offered me no protection from the haunts.

"The water's rising..." The teasing, disembodied whisper of a sailor who drowned. It sailed past me like sea foam in a storm.

My heart slewed sideways. Drowning at sea was the only thing I feared worse than the ghosts.

I fixed my eyes to the far hatch.

Just keep walking.

The floor pitched against each step. Working in the windowless dark, I'd learnt to read each motion of the ship and today I sensed the ocean outside was wild—no calm sea to give us easy passage.

Everything was off kilter today.

It seemed an age before the cold, steel hatch-wheel was in my grip. I breathed out a sigh and turned it. The door seal cracked. Light spilled across the threshold as I stepped into another corridor, this one wide, bright, and gleaming, made for the cleaner work belonging to officers and bridge crew. Here, the walls were transparent, revealing the working innards of the vessel. Beautiful and complicated, the copper and gold clockwork mechanisms whirred and wound behind their sheets of hardened glass.

"Blood on the cogs…"

I swivelled with a tight intake of breath. An older ghost stood by my shoulder, his soul so threadbare as to be almost colourless. Yet his touch held strength as he raked the memory of his yellowed nails across my throat. Goosebumps rippled down my arms. Then he retreated, pointing left. I turned. The cogs in the walls dripped with ephemeral blood and viscera. A transparent, mangled corpse—face torn and limbs jammed—leered at me.

A man who'd died in the walls.

I shook off the ghost's touch with a growl and headed for the bridge.

The captain's voice was loud even through the steel door. Deep and sonorous, he barked commands to his crew. I entered the room quietly, marvelling at the grace and curvature of the gleaming instruments that lined the consoles. The elegant compass nestled in its cradle of gold and brass next to the navigational officer's station. Captain Reed stood, legs braced before the polished wooden wheel, broad-ended fingers curled around the walnut timber spokes that guided the rudder. But for me, the true beauty lay outside the vessel. As always, on the rare occasion I was called to this lofty station, my attention was drawn to the large expanse of glass that overlooked the tarnished brass smoke-stacks, the iron-sheet deck and ocean. And I was right. Today the sea was bleak, a wash of grey beneath an even greyer sky. Waves, tops thrashed to white, buffeted the horizon. A storm was on its way. A bad one.

The ghosts muttered, "The water is rising. Blood on the cogs…"

"Stoker Webb." Captain Reed's level gaze held mine, his hands resting lightly on the wheel.

I saluted. "Reporting, as requested, sir."

Reed nodded. "How much coal have we left in the hold, son?"

This was something Zeke would know. Why hadn't the captain asked him? I swallowed my annoyance. "Almost empty, Captain, but we're on track to make it to port."

Reed's dark brows furrowed over his eagle-sharp nose. "It won't be enough."

I glanced at the gathering storm. "Sir?"

Reed frowned. "Back to your post, son. Stoke the furnace to full and make it hot. We need everything out of these engines. There's blood on the cogs and the water's rising."

Those words again...

Then Reed turned away.

I stumbled back, eyes wide.

The captain had a great, gaping wound cut across his spine.

He's dead—I'm only seeing his shade. I glanced around the rest of the crew and my stomach dropped.

They were all dead too.

But only newly so. For while their edges were transparent, their eyes and souls still retained colour and form. Like the captain, some of the crew showed the wounds that killed them—throats slit, others with worse.

It was only now I noticed the floor wetted with gore, scarlet and not yet congealed.

But no corpses.

What the hell had happened here?

The whole ghostly crew stopped and considered me.

Outside, the ship powered into the growing waves.

I couldn't help it.

I ran.

———

My vomit splattered hot and acrid across the corridor. The smell of the crew's blood clung to me, and no amount of clearing my throat seemed to loosen it.

Zeke. I had to get back to him. As much as I hated him, he deserved to be warned. I wiped my mouth on my sleeve and sprinted down the corridor, headed for the stokehold hatch. Around me, the cogs in the walls continued to turn.

The ghosts appeared ahead of me, forming a line to bar the path. Damn it. I brushed through them, the cold tatters of their souls clinging to my shirt as I raced to my post.

I slammed open the hatch. "Zeke!"

Silence held the room, thick and heavy like felt. I stumbled to the furnace. The grate hung open and the fire burned low. The ghosts crowded in behind me. Frantic, I grabbed a discarded shovel and piled on extra fuel. Slowly, it ignited, licks of flame catching to the coal.

The spirits grudgingly retreated.

Where was Zeke?

I hung my shovel, took a kerosene lamp from its hook by the rack, and headed deeper into the stoke-hold where the furnace's belly roared and piles of coal spilled across the floor. My boots slipped on the uneven surface. The ghosts flanked me but kept their distance. Their dark, hollow eyes followed my every move.

An empty kerosine tin rolled across my path. Things always move in a ship, especially as it pitched and yawed through a storm. But this movement was different. The tin didn't roll back, instead remaining pressed to the far wall. The floor…it leaned as if the ship had settled to port.

A ghost sailor, dressed in an old stoker's uniform, stepped in and swiped at my lamp. It dropped from my fingers, the glass shattering as it rolled to settle by the tin. The small flame stuttered yet remained burning low on the wick, offering just enough light to see by, but not to deter the spirits.

"The water is rising…" whispered the phantom.

I lunged for the lamp and retrieved it. The wick extended and light bloomed out. The ghost retreated and I swallowed. With the ship's deck at this angle, it was clear we were taking on water.

What do I do?

A dark, sticky-looking trail smeared on the deck caught my attention. I leaned in, the firelight revealing blood slicked across the floor.

My hand shook. The light trembled.

A secondary door led from the rear of the stoke-hold through to the older corridors giving access to the engine room. I followed the blood. Shadows pressed close. The smell of salt and old oil grew stronger here, underpinned by darker notes of grief and half-remembered terrors. I tried to ignore the threads of sorrow and memory leached by the ship, just as insidious as the ghosts who never left me be.

The steady rumble of the engines drew me on. They grew louder as I neared. Ahead, the hatch stood ajar, beckoning. How could an exit look so hungry? My heart clenched into a knot, tighter than a fist. I swallowed spit soured by fear and stepped through.

The next corridor was shadowed, not having the same expensive electric bulbs that were installed in the ones above. The small light offered by my lamp was just enough to illuminate the black-red trail I followed.

The body of a mid-shipman materialised out of the gloom. Blond-haired and slight of frame, his throat was cut, and not neatly. The death stroke was a ragged score on the column of his neck—a disturbing contrast to his bloodied but otherwise neat uniform. I pressed a hand to my mouth. He wasn't much older than me.

The ship lurched further to port and I stumbled against the wall. An ominous groan echoed through the metal. Time was running out.

I slid past the boy just as his soul separated from his corpse. He looked confused as he ran a pale hand through his fringe and then touched the wound on his throat. We made eye contact and his lips moved, but I didn't wait to either listen or explain. I left him to cry over his own corpse.

The hull groaned again and I could all but feel the heavy press of water against the steel—the ocean's desire to flood the compartments and claim the ship, to deliver death by drowning.

The thought of the crushing depths and crabs nibbling at my flesh...I just needed to find Zeke and then get the hell off this ship.

The door to the engine room was closed. With the angle of the deck, its heavy metal construction kept it firmly pressed against the seals.

I battled the weight and forced my way inside. The room was lit with strings of electric lights that flickered like moths. The air boiled hot as the engine's main cogs and steam-driven valves churned away, their thunderous voices an assault on the senses.

Adjusting my hold on the lamp, I circled around the closest of the great piston housings and skirted beneath one of three gleaming mechanisms. The air down here smelled damp. Years of engine steam and oil had conspired to make the floor slick. My boots slipped, and I swear the deck was trying to trip me. I turned a corner and found the water.

It poured in through a series of holes punched through the side of the ship. The metal shards of the wounds curled outward, the damage made from within rather than from anything the sea threw at us. Salt water and foam gushed through them like blood pouring from a torn artery.

Who would have done such a terrible thing?

The water is rising...

Terror surged; adrenaline powered me. No longer worried about Zeke but with thoughts turned to the lifeboats lashed to the decks above, I ran, distress at the rising water greater than my fear of the ghosts. Overhead, the clockwork cogs turned and turned, their cadence beating as if to measure the last moments of my life. I visualised the open sky, a picture of white caps on a vast ocean, and I held tight to that image.

Zeke was waiting for me at the hatch, eyes wild

and teeth bared. He stood braced against the floor's tilt, machete gripped in his meaty hand.

"Zeke? What are you doing?"

"It ends here, Gypsy Boy," he snarled, and then lunged.

I pushed the blade aside. A sting to the palm; the keen blade nicked my flesh. Zeke's free hand snapped forward and caught me around the throat. I swung at his chest, but my punches landed on flesh hardened by a lifetime before the furnace. I couldn't break free.

He leaned in. "Got one final job for you."

I sucked stunted breaths as he dragged me toward the heart of the engine, the place where the largest of the cogs whirred to keep the ship's rudders steady. A slaughterhouse stench rose, hanging concentrated in the air—death and body fluids.

"There's blood on the cogs..."

The ghost's whispers filled my mind as Zeke threw me face down across a metal beam and bound my hands to it.

I glanced up and wished I hadn't.

Above me rotated the rudder cogs. Their usually gleaming surfaces were ragged and stained. To each of the great spokes was tied the corpse of a crew member. Torn flesh hung from stiffened limbs, and those still with eyes stared blankly into the darkness.

"Time for you to join the rest of the crew," said Zeke, his breath hot against my ear.

"What have you done?" I whispered.

"Can't your ghost friends tell you?"

The haunts, as if summoned, appeared from thin air. They gathered, solemn, below the hanging corpses. Captain Reed stepped forward, hand outstretched.

"Fear the living," he said to me. "They're the monsters here."

I glanced at Zeke, "You murdered them, Chief?" I asked, horrified. "All of them! Why?"

Zeke's gaze darkened like a sea horizon before a storm. "You wouldn't understand."

"No? Try me, you son of a bitch!"

Zeke snarled and slammed the flat of his machete against a piston casing. The ring of distressed steel clamoured, discordant. Then he closed his eyes. When he opened them, bloodshot sclera ringed his irises—a gaze wild, angry, and murderous.

Something was broken inside of Zeke.

He snapped his teeth at me, like a shark tasting blood in the water.

Then he threw a hand up in the air, palm stained with coal dust. "I signed up to be a sailor, but instead of fighting for my country, I was put into the belly of this iron beast and have since spent a lifetime feeding it coal. No clean breeze on my brow, only darkness, dust, and terror. Haven't you felt it? The way it bleeds out of the walls and into your skull?" Zeke smacked his palm against his temple. "You asked me once if I could see ghosts. I can't, but maybe it's them I feel. In my head. And they're always in the stokehold. Just them, the furnace, and those four steel walls."

He swung his machete. The edge gleamed silver in the lamplight. "I can't fuckin' take it anymore!"

"Please, Zeke, you don't have to do this."

"But I do. I've given everything to the Navy. But no more. This crew died so Chief Stoker Zeke Marshall could die. The old Zeke will go down with this ship. Tomorrow, I'll be a new man, and I'll be far, far away. Away from the fear, away from the coal dust, away from these damn walls."

"You're crazy."

"No. I'm smart. Because unlike you, I'm getting off this tub."

"Please...*please* don't kill me."

Zeke frowned. "You won't die by my hand. You worked hard at the furnace, same as me. I respect that. You can stick around to see the end." He knelt and ensured the knots against my wrist were tight. Satisfied, he stood. "See ya, kid."

His footsteps were lost to the groans of the dying

ship. I struggled against my bonds but it was useless. The deck pitched higher and the water first lapped at my feet, then soon reached my chin. I sobbed. Strained to lift my head. The sea kissed my nostrils.

My ghosts gathered close and for the first time, I was thankful for their presence. At least I wasn't alone.

One by one, each haunt touched a hand to my shoulder, fingertips freezing. My breaths came rapid and shallow. I gripped the beam with both hands, took courage from the iron, and wondered if it, even at the bottom of the ocean, would hold the memory of my death.

The ship groaned as she settled deeper into the ocean's embrace. The engine's bite-toothed cogs finally whirred to a stop, the corpses they held slumped against their bonds. Then the water closed over my head.

I held my breath for as long as I could but soon the briny liquid scored its way into my lungs.

The ghosts whispered to me one last time.

"The water has risen," they said, "and the cogs are washed clean."

OF SLAVES AND LIONS

These ruined gardens were once beautiful. But the wide manicured paths I remember have faded to tracks and the friendly trees have changed. Their crowns look heavy, bristling with dead twigs earned from too many seasons of neglect. I walk with my head down, loathe to tarry. The desire to settle a score with the ghosts of my past is my focus. I stride on, hoping to hear them, but they are yet to speak.

An overgrown hedge of bougainvillea bars my way. Bright bunches of purple flowers hang from the vines. Thorns pluck at my sleeves and cheeks as I pass through. The greenery gives way to a clearing and a ring of dead trees. An ancient pond resides at their centre. The silence of the gardens stifles. No crickets chirruping, no birdsong. There is only the riot of colourful flowers from overgrown vines and stillness like a neglected graveyard.

The old pond sits dead. The bowl is dry and the low wall surrounding it is all but consumed by a heavily-scented jasmine vine. This was my favourite place to play as a child. But alike to that childhood, it has been reduced to bones. I swallow my disappointment. This was the last place I recall being happy. A part of me hoped it had survived. I take a moment to imagine bright fish flitting through the cool water and the vibrancy of the yellow water lilies that once grew here.

Daylight is wasting. Time to continue on if I wish to make the hike back to King's Highway and my horse before dusk. Beyond the trees, the mouldering walls of the old castle rise like broken teeth into the sky. Long ago that castle was my home. I am hesitant to approach it. Do I wish to enter there and see again those stones stained with blood? I set aside the horror, remind myself again of my purpose. There must be something of my past—something good—still lingering here.

The pond and its debris-filled bowl falls away behind me. The heady scent of jasmine rises as I disturb the vine. The perfume curls around me, reminding me of warmer, friendlier days filled with sunlight and laughter. The heaviness in my heart eases just a bit.

My reverie is broken. The first sound I've heard in this place since I arrived reaches my ears.

A growl. Low. Fierce.

It comes from the densest part of the shrubbery by the pond, where the greenery covering the wall piles up higher than everywhere else. I ease closer, hesitant. Then I see *her.*

A lioness. She is trapped in a rusted cage—one of the old traps my father's gardener used to set for wolves in the castle grounds. The great cat's eyes gleam, furious. She strikes at the bars. I fall back as her long claws screech down the metal. She retreats to the rear of her prison, her ears held flat to her head and her lips wrinkled back, exposing the pointed lengths of her yellow teeth.

How did such a creature find her way into this garden? Then I remember the new king's lion pits located just outside the city, the pits where the underprivileged are tossed when they fail to pay their tithes. Perhaps she came from there; a lioness with a taste for human flesh.

I lean in closer. She snarls a low warning. Her fierce, yellow gaze holds mine, conveying a message. *I am a fighter, a survivor. I live beyond the rules men would impose on me.*

Her message resonates.

This cat's soul is a mirror of my own.

And she is abandoned in this palace, just as I once was. My thoughts turn back to the day my childhood ended. At the height of summer, a dry and dusty heat had settled over the gardens. It was the day my father threw away everything. I hadn't understood what it meant when he assembled his soldiers and left through the front gate. But I learnt soon enough. The rebels were coming. And when they arrived, even at the tender age of nine, I saw the truth. My father left us because he feared his own death more than he loved his family and his people. Not that it helped him. The rebel king's forces captured him in the mountains a few months later.

My mother, the queen, was different. She died the day he left. But I still recall her strength. She had only just hidden me under her bed when the rebels found her. She never betrayed me as they tore the jewels from her neck and ripped her silken gown. And worse. I wish I were more my mother's daughter, but my life has been lived on the edge of a knife —a brutal, hard existence. I am the reverse side of her card. My anger and grief have twisted me. My everyday struggle is to find a place of equanimity.

I brush away the tatters of old memories and the

rage they re-awaken. My hope is still to find peace in this return to my childhood home.

The lioness growls again. She wants out, but how to release her? I could leave her here, let her perish. What would be the point of dying trying to save her?

The animal paces. Her yellow hide dapples in the thin sunlight, reaching past the thick bars and the jasmine's runaway foliage.

Again I am reminded of myself. I paced like that, paced after the rebels captured me and tossed me in a different type of cage…

My decision is made. I'll not leave the cat locked away without a fighting chance.

I'll set her free.

Just like I was set free, albeit scarred and broken and angry. I was saved from my slave-pit cage by the kindness of my father's old gardener. It'd been a long time—ten years since she last saw me, since I was captured and sent to work in the new king's brothels.

She'd paused too when she saw me.

I could smell her fear.

But she handed over the gold to free me.

And like her, I am nothing if not compassionate.

I search for something to loosen the rusted drop-pin holding the door closed. A windfall of weathered branches leaning against the pond looks promising. I pull a thick length of timber free, a length hardened in sunlight and silvered with the passage of years.

It hits the drop-pin with a sharp crack and no luck.

The lioness shies away from the sound, retreating to the far corner of the cage. Her eyes glitter as she watches me—me, the girl who was once a princess, but now just a freed slave with a stick. Malevolence drips from the great cat's stare.

Another hit. The lioness skids to the other side of the cage, her ears flat again. The end of the branch shatters as I miss and connect with the side of the cage. A shower of splinters falls onto the leaf litter below. My palm stings from the backlash; I shake my hand and aim again.

This time I hit the pin with a solid thud. The force of the blow slips it free, letting it fall to the ground in a curtain of rust.

The door creaks open an inch. The lioness's gaze slews sideways to the gap in the cage. I shuffle my grip on the branch, ready to use it as a club if I must.

The lioness pads to the door. Cautious. Her golden hide is crisscrossed with raised ridges of pink flesh, a patchwork of fur and knotted seams. I have seen enough battle scars in my lifetime to recognize the work of a sword at play.

Someone somewhere fought this lioness.

I wonder if they survived.

The great cat hesitates by the door. Her predator's stare follows me—that unblinking gaze of molten gold shot through with black. Taking a breath, I step forward. Slipping the end of my branch through the bars, I pull the door wider. It shrieks on unoiled hinges.

The piercing noise is my undoing. Startled, my attention slips.

The lioness reacts, a streak of gold and muscle flying past the open door and into the ruined garden of my childhood. She skids to a stop behind me, scattering leaf litter and debris across the ground. Her claws are out, thick black hooks that clutch at the earth. Her gaze trains on me, locked like a vice. Her throat ripples. A low growl rolls out into the autumn air.

Perhaps talk will make a difference. "You're free. Go!"

The lioness's growl deepens. Her gaze slips to the club in my hand. The weapon.

I glance at it and then back at her. At her tattered hide and the hatred that burns so bright in her bearing. Realization dawns.

Broken souls are not saved by brutality or bloodshed.

I lean down and place the branch on the ground. The lioness' gaze follows every movement. My hand trembles as I hold it out in front of me, naked.

The dry grass crackles beneath my feet as I move toward the lioness. The tip of my boot scatters a loose stone. Another step. The lioness's haunches bunch. I don't dare pause, afraid my new resolve will waver.

My fingers hover inches away from the great cat. I do not presume to touch, but stand and let her choose to close the distance. My heart hammers in my chest. It's hard to breathe.

I close my eyes and wait. As I do, I realise the garden has awoken. It is full of sound. I focus on the distant birdsong, the crickets and the gentle breeze playing through the trees.

The lioness's touch is tentative at first, just a brush of warmth against my palm. But then she presses harder. I open my eyes. The cat's chin rests in my open hand. Her eyes are on me, but the hate is gone. There is only trust.

I smile, the first genuine one in ten years, and wonder on the strangeness of fate—a fate in which a battered slave tames a savage beast. But perhaps not so strange. It is the lesson my mother died teaching me: that strength is not always about how hard you hit, but how immense your heart can be.

I hold the lioness and turn my gaze to the sky. The broken sunlight kisses my cheeks and with its touch, I find resolution.

I have found my ghosts and they have spoken.

KEEP THE STITCHES SMALL

To make a soul, the pieces must be cut from rolls of stardust. The slices need to be clean and the stitches to fashion them into shape must be small. Around the ankles and the wrists. Around the neck. The threads I use are precious and rare. Carefully prepared by the old gods, before they fell to fire and ruin, each strand gifts a quality: Luck, or Happiness, or Grief. Once, I would have stitched in Love to balance the mix, but those spools stand empty, the threads used long ago.

I spread a piece of star-fabric and smooth it. My shears cut the slippery weave like hot coals through ice, and a piece separates—a torso, emerging as if it were only waiting for its excess to be slewed away. This soul is smaller than those I fashioned in ages past. For as my thread stock diminishes, I ensure there is no excess space. Humanity already shoulders enough emptiness.

I reach for a needle, a filament of scarlet running from the eye. For this soul, to replace the lack of Love, I choose to weave in a little more Courage. This one's spirit will dominate, large enough to encompass the world. She will be a warrior daughter to champion the masses—a soul for the ages.

I lean in close to keep the stitches small.

With the line across her breast complete, I knot and break the thread, tasting bitterness against my lips. That will not do, and I see my error—too much spirit can turn sour. With my calloused thumb, I smooth over the end torn by my yellowed teeth and twist a knot of Compassion into the thread. I am hoping this will lend a more honeyed disposition, strong but sweet. A soul respected by all who meet her.

I stretch my shoulders, easing the ache from stiffened joints. I blink and my vision blurs. A thousand years I have been at this work, at this stitching of stardust and souls. Such fine craftsmanship is demanding, and age has taken its toll. I feel the threads of my divine purpose always looming—stretching out across eternity—but I cannot rest, not yet. Humankind flourishes under the banners of bountiful abundance, and while they breed, I will continue to sew.

Time to stitch the eyes. My coloured spools of thread are lined like soldiers along the shelf beside me. For this creation, I want something special. I choose slate grey to craft eyes of Power that radiate like a stormfront cresting an ocean's back. I pause, thinking, then add a rare thread of gold to my selection—because gold is the sun, and the sun is Promise, always rising after a storm.

Keep the stitches small.

Grey. Black. Gold. Eyes are the most difficult element to craft, the patterns in each one as unique as a fingerprint. My melancholy and weariness leaches into my work. I frown, upset that I have tainted the stitches. To recalibrate the design, I choose a cobalt blue thread of Spiritualism—just a dash added to each eye. Now this soul will see beyond the veil of reality. She will know that happiness lingers past my infectious sorrow. I tie Caution into the final knot. A necessary safeguard. Experience has taught me that unrestrained spirituality turns to madness under the weight of sighted knowledge.

Snip and smooth. From the eyes, I leave two clear

threads hanging, Emotion to be later tied into the heart. And this one's heart? I choose green thread, to foster the love of Wild Places. This soul will run barefoot over mountains, dew-soaked feet dancing on clouds. I am halfway through when I realise I haven't enough green. With a sigh, I pick up mustard yellow—Longing. A shame. Now, this child will dream of green places but will never dwell there.

My mistakes are mounting. Have I ruined this soul already, having denied it so much? When did I start making such foolish decisions?

Do I give up trying and set this creation aside?

I frown. This soul is not what I intended it to be. She is a patchwork of conflicting colours, a mismatched collection of threads. But the stitches are stitched, and they are small and neat. I can only move forward. I draw a fortifying breath and gather up the loose, clear threads and tie them into the soul's heart knot. Instantly the strings swell and turn white. My breath hitches. Milk is the colour of Destiny. A rare and unexpected phenomenon that cannot ever be foreseen or manufactured.

Why has it presented here and now?

A rattle sounds at my chamber door. I glance up as it opens of its own accord, revealing a view to the shifting grey clouds of chaos outside. From the eternal storm stalks my friend, Sphinx. Her wings, feathered tips streaming aether, gleam copper in the lamplight, the sparks of Immortality woven through them rippling like distant constellations. Smart, hard, and merciless, she is a creature from another age, one that no longer has a place in the modern world. Her soul was sewn by my predecessor, Arachne, and the work is exquisite.

Sphinx moves closer, claws clicking on stone tiles.

"You are getting old, Yfantis. Your stitches are not as clean as they once were." Her words sound like venomous barbs, but I take no offence. She has Love, but no Tact in her weave.

I nod, for the criticism is truth. "We are both getting old."

"Magic sustains me. What do you have?"

I knot a thread. "Purpose."

"Ha! You are a flawed creation."

"Arachne did the best with what she had."

"You are a symbol of her Vanity. Nothing more."

Never Vanity. Arachne, weaver goddess—the last old-world goddess to fall in the war against the younger, rising gods of men—knew what was needed when she fashioned me. Without an entity to stich souls, humanity would die out. I am flawed, but I am the custodian of human nature—the prodigy of a dying goddess who in her last moments gathered the charred threads of Purpose clinging to her battle-blooded skirts and stitched me to life.

And her last gift to seal my ascension were the threads she gave from herself, those that shine brightest in my own weave, being Duty, Love, and Perseverance.

I thread another needle with the bright purple of Grace and press the tip to the soul's brow.

Sphinx circles me, her cold face smooth as porcelain, her gaze as fierce as a forge.

"Your purpose is obsolete, old woman. Your spools are almost empty. Let humanity die out so we can own the world. I will take the skies and you can roam the lands."

The years have certainly depleted my stocks. "They're not empty yet."

Sphinx cackles. "You are a fool."

"So you like to remind me. But I riddle you this… Two immortals, and one without Purpose is doomed to fade to nothing. What will you do when you are left alone?"

Sphinx frowns. "Do not riddle a Riddlemaster."

I smile to myself. Sphinx thinks she can hide Fear from me, but I see the vermillion filaments stitched into her flanks.

"Besides," I say, "even if humanity was to pass, the

younger gods would defy us. They spend all their time hunting me. They would never let us walk free in the world."

Sphinx scoffs. "We should stop hiding. You should let me challenge them. Their magic is weak, their hold on this universe tenuous."

"We are all that is left of the old world, Sphinx, and more, you are too important to me. I fear their cruel and devious natures."

"They are no match for us."

Her faith warms me. "Perhaps one day we will challenge them together."

"Spoken like a spider who likes hiding in her workshop."

"Spoken like a spoilt, petulant child."

"Ha!" Sphinx, typically enjoying such discourse, smiles.

I sit back from my work, the soul laid out on my workbench now complete. I gently touch the glowing lines of stitching that hold the stardust pieces together, ensuring they sit smooth. The ephemeral planes of this soul's form already hint at the person she will become. Due to my inadequate skill, I suspect she will suffer great loneliness, and while I am sorry for that, I also know she will bring true greatness to the world.

"Let's send her on her way."

Sphinx remains silent. She recognises the gravity of what comes next.

I breathe out over my creation, ancient notes of music that caress life into existence. The soul begins to glow, shimmering with vitality. I lift my hands and make ready to guide her out into the universe.

"Wait. I smell something," whispers Sphinx.

I pause. Sphinx's eyes are trained on the closed door. A shadow moves outside, visible under the bottom edge.

"Who is there?" I call.

The door swings open. Outside, the shifting chaos roils, then darkens. A man dressed in a green pinstripe suit steps from it, crossing the threshold, and while I take no interest in the young gods, this one's reputation precedes him.

"Yfantis." Greed's stance bleeds arrogance. "You're a hard soul to find."

I lower my hands. "Only when I have no wish to be found."

Greed grins, his uneven teeth sharpened to scarlet points. "Are you ready to relinquish dominion over the souls of Earth?"

Sphinx hisses.

I press my palms to my benchtop. Greed has the right to challenge me, as does any god or goddess, but the ancient rules must be followed.

"To earn your place at this bench," I say, "you must answer Sphinx's riddle."

Greed laughs, the sound like tin cans pouring into polluted water. "This is a modern world. The rules set by dead gods don't apply anymore. I'll just take what I want."

Sphinx stalks forward, her wings held wide and arched in challenge. "Answer or die," she says.

Greed tilts his head. "I don't think so."

He clenches his right fist and squeezes; the tendons writhe like bloated maggots, tighter and tighter until the skin on his forearm splits. Blood, green as poison, pours from the wound. It spatters to my floor, steaming as it etches deep into the stone.

I glare at him but hold my tongue. This arena belongs to Sphinx—her Purpose, as defined by the old gods, resonates in this moment.

Greed licks his lips and his blood coalesces. The dreadful threads gather in his cupped hand and in moments form the flat grey construct of a human gun.

Straightening the gore-slick muzzle, he aims it at Sphinx.

"It's time you both join the gods who left you here."

Sphinx moves like mercury—too fast for Greed

to react. Her copper claws, curved like scythes, extend as she launches for Greed. She tears away the side of his face, flesh flaying in a spray of acid green. Greed howls, clutching the wound. His eyes spark an unnatural red, a red born of electricity, wires, and technology. The colour reveals his nature to me, a soul stitched in corrupted lines of Oil and Coal, fashioned by the stone needles of slain continents.

Greed's broad hand circles Sphinx's throat. She keens a choked-off cry, and her pain dims the brightness of her liquid gold and ebony eyes.

Desperate, I grasp a handful of needles. The terror that she will be ended, and that I will be alone, burns my stomach sour. With a thrust, I drive the needles into Greed's side. He stumbles but straightens, and too late I see that unthreaded, such meagre weapons hold no power to slow him.

Sphinx coughs—the sound of age-old bedrock breaking—and her perfect stitches, as woven by Arachne, shear apart. My friend's Immortality bleeds out her mouth and across Greed's hand, silver threaded through with ultramarine and ruby.

Sphinx slumps.

Her last breath, retched out across Greed's knuckles, is the testament to my eternal heartbreak.

Rage surges, a cascade of blind emotion, and with it I conceive the unthinkable. Caution thrown to the wind, I tear down the shelf holding my spools. My precious, irreplaceable threads spill across the floor, heavy with the qualities held within them. I raise my voice and sing them to life. Not stitched into stardust, the strands become serpents.

Greed screams as fiery orange filaments of Hate encircle him. He struggles as the ocean blue of Sorrow coils up into his mouth and crawls down his throat. And still I sing. I call the light grey threads of Oblivion and the deep onyx of Death and bury them into his eyes. His corrupted soul pours from the ruined sockets and spiders down his ravaged cheeks, and I delight in his downfall.

And then cocooned in all the threads he topples, dead, to the floor.

Through the open chamber door, mutters rise. But the other younger gods lingering outside are cowards. None are brave enough to show their face.

I cross the floor and gather the remaining unspooled threads into my hands. Sphinx's immortal blood has soaked through some, turning them luminous. My tears fall to them and the colours begin to run. Red into yellow and blue into green, all the myriad qualities that define humankind blurring into one. I bend my head and hold the ruined threads to my brow.

A gentle hand touches my shoulder.

I look up. My throat closes over. The last soul I stitched. She survives.

And amid sorrow, I find a grain of joy. Because I see that for all this soul's imperfections, her stitches are small and clean in their creation. And that line of Destiny, unforeseen, but so strong where it ties into her heart—

I know the reason for it now.

I reach into my chest and grasp the small, most precious thread Arachne gave me. I pull Love free, gasping at its sudden loss. I hold it up and the soul nods, gathering it in her delicate fingers. She bends her head and winds it around her own heart. Then from my ruined bench, she selects a needle threaded with Purpose. With dutiful care, she stitches my gift into place. And like Arachne before me, I pass my burden onto a fresh soul.

It is with great pride that I see my successor keeping her stitches small.

With the last thread tied, the soul knots it with Duty and turns away from me, ready to begin the ages of work to come. Alone, I kneel by Sphinx. Her body has cooled and stiffened in death. I smooth back her hair and tuck her sprawled wings closed. I wipe the smears of Immortality from her lips and press a final kiss to her unlined brow. Already her edges are fading and, like myself, soon she will pass into myth. So long we have been together. So long. I lay down on the floor and wrap my arms around her. As my own stitches begin to unravel, I close my eyes and imagine we own the world. I see Sphinx soaring through clear skies and for myself, I take the wooded paths stitched through verdant lands.

BONES TO FEED FALLOW FIELDS

It's said these cursed mountains devour men, but I find they eat women just as often. Either way, it matters not to me, for bones are bones, and bones are money, and I am nothing if not a woman who covets gold.

My horse, Kita, knows these treacherous paths. She navigates the sparse, dead forests with ease, passing the ethereal silvered trees that stand with shattered limbs twisted by the wind. Sometimes, when the melancholy mood overtakes me, I imagine they are weeping for those who have died in these lands.

I hum as we travel, skirting the snowline, letting Kita choose the way—the horse has a nose for finding the dead. And she doesn't fail me. She soon halts, head held high, ears pressed forward. She huffs, her breath clouding to mist in the chilled air.

"What is it, my love?" I ask.

She tosses her head, front hoof pawing the barren, stony ground.

Death. Bones.

"Good girl."

I slide from the saddle. My pots, tied from the horn, rattle as I knock them with my shoulder. I unhook my collection sack beside them. The bones I've already collected today clatter, those of an eagle and a native dog we found on our way up. I shoulder the bag and circle Kita. I can't see what she senses, but I can smell it—the sweet-rot scent of decomposition coming from the tumble of boulders next to the path.

Flies rise in a cloud from the corpse I find sprawled behind the rocks. The carcass is badly decomposed, but it's human—a male, or at least I think it is, the body being far taller and slimmer than anything I've seen before. A nest of long, tangled brown hair still clings to the grinning skull, a skull armed with teeth broader and longer than any human has the right to own. I'm sorry to see the demise of a fellow traveller, but bones are bones. I drop my sack to the ground and pull my filleting knife from my belt. The bones are no use unless cleaned, so I ready to remove the flesh before I boil them down.

Kita, picketed by the nearest tree, sidles as I add another log to my campfire. Smoke and sparks curl up into the evening, ethereal strokes against the night's indigo sky. I lean back on my saddlebags and watch the pot slowly boil over low flames, the water melting the last shreds of meat from the bones. I ruminate on the strangeness of the man they belonged to. Cleaning them, while typically unpleasant, had revealed a strange, vitrified smoothness to their lengths. The bones almost seem crafted of glass rather than the typical porous material I grind down to sell to the valley folk—folk who pay good money to purchase the rare powder to fertilise their fields.

I pick up my stick and lean over to stir the pot. The bones clink, again like glass. I begin to wonder if these will even grind down properly.

"I'm not sure what you found for us this time, Kita," I mumble.

The fire cracks and a log shifts. I jump and the mare pulls against her tether. The light catches her long nose and casts her eyes into ghoulish shadows.

"It's just the fire, girl. Rest easy."

But she remains vigilant, gaze fixed to a point somewhere past the treeline. Her intensity raises the hairs on my neck. This night has eyes. I'm sure of it.

Another crack, this time from the forest behind me. I turn. The tall, bone-white trees loom, their twisted limbs holding back a curtain of darkness.

I recline back and ease the dagger from the sheath at my hip. I lock my fingers on the hilt. A breeze kicks up and the tree limbs rattle. They sound like my collection bag does when it's full. I keep an eye on the forest.

"Anyone out there?" I call.

The dry grasses shift in a sudden breeze.

"Just a traveller."

I swivel—blade up, edge catching the firelight.

A young woman walks into camp. Her eyes, luminous blue, seem so much older than her smooth face suggests. She holds her hands up, empty.

"May I share your fire?" she asks.

My hand tightens on the hilt. People don't just wander around in the dark up here, so close to the summit.

She smiles and fine wrinkles crinkle at the corners of her eyes. "Surely you don't fear a fellow woman, out past dark and travelling alone?"

I take in her tall, thin form, her patchwork cloak. She looks as if she would blow over in a stiff wind.

Cautious, I nod to the opposite side of the flames. "You can join me to catch your breath, but you can't stay."

"The rest alone is welcome."

The woman circles. She glances briefly at the pot and then sits.

"I'm hungry," she says.

"That isn't food."

"What then?"

I lay my knife across my knee, close to hand. "Bones. I'm a bone collector."

"A bone collector?"

"I gather them off the mountain to sell for profit." I shrug. "Some folk believe the ground-down powder brings good luck when tilled into food-bearing earth."

The woman frowns. "And what about the mountain? If you take the bones and his good luck from him, how is he to remain bountiful?" She scans the dead trees. "Maybe you have already taken too much."

I chuckle. "It's all nonsense." I tap the purse tied to my belt. "It's gold that holds power in this world, and the bones bring me that."

"Gold?"

"Yes."

"So, you swap bones for gold."

"Yes."

"And you don't see the irony in that?"

"Irony?"

"The mountain's own bedrock—its bones—are made of gold. You sell bones for bones."

Something about the way she says it suggests I should be ashamed. But outcast women like myself have two options to make a living. I choose the one that allows me freedom.

I lift my chin. "I only deal with the dead. Gold is metal. It's not a living part of the mountain."

The woman nods and looks to the pot. Her eerie eyes catch the firelight, turning them to moonstones.

"I understand."

I shift, uncomfortable. I wish to be rid of her company. Maybe if I share food, she'll leave sooner. "Here." I reach into my saddle pack and hold out a pouch of dried apple. "It isn't much but you're welcome to it."

The woman reaches over and takes the food. Her skin brushes mine. I jerk back my hand. She is cold to touch, her fingers like ice.

She glances at me and smiles again. "Thank you."

I rub my palm to warm it, but the more I rub, the colder my skin feels. I hold my hand out to the fire, but the warmth feeds the uncanny sensation. The cold rises, creeping up into my wrist and forearm. It reaches my neck and my tongue.

I try to speak but the words are locked in my frozen throat.

Confused, I look to the woman.

She sits quietly, eyes gleaming as she chews thoughtfully on the apple.

Kita nickers and paws the ground.

Why is my mare sensing death?

The woman is stronger than she looks. I'm helpless as she lifts my rigid body from the fireside. Kita calls after me as we pass her, but I cannot answer.

I try to struggle but in vain. My breaths quicken as we travel higher up the mountain, up through the dark and over bare stones.

Where is she taking me?

We hit the snowline and continue on, the woman's footsteps turning from the crunch of dead brushwood into the squeak of new snow underfoot. And still we climb, headed, it seems, for the summit.

It's when dawn crests in the eastern sky, a canvas of orange and purple, that we reach the plateau. The woman drops me to the snow, hard enough that my teeth clatter. I blink—the only movement I control—

as the thin, cold air brushes my brow and lips. I again try to move but remain wooden.

Humming fills the air, a sweet melody that brings to mind wide blue vistas, heady thunderstorms, and wild valleys that drop into shadow. A quiet rattle underpins the song—the sound of bones tumbling from my sack onto the snow.

"An eagle, a dog, and the Spirit of the Mountain. Quite the haul, bone collector."

My captor steps into my field of view. Her hair blooms around her head, the new rays of morning sunlight crowning her in gold. Her eyes stare into mine, unblinking.

"You took, and took, the bones from these mountains. You took until *his* lands starved. And then when the Mountain Spirit—my brother—had nothing left to give and he died, you flayed the flesh from his bones and boiled them in your *pot*."

Her spittle lands on my cheek and freezes there.

Who is this woman?

She must read the question in my gaze.

"I am the Spirit of the Skies, and I am most unmerciful."

Sweat breaks out on the back of my neck. I would whimper if I could.

The deity swings away from me, her cloak swirling snowflakes like powder. She retrieves the fallen bones and lays them around me. The skulls she positions on my chest and abdomen.

"Now you will give back what you took."

My stomach sours.

The sky-woman slams her fist through the snow. I hear her knuckles hit the bedrock and crack like thunder. She snarls, baring her teeth, and they are broad and long like her brother's—teeth, not quite human, but at home in the mouths of gods.

Tears streak her face as she mutters strange words into the bitter wind cresting the razorback plateau's rim. The ground beneath me warms. At first, I welcome the heat—the sensation of thawing—but then I begin to burn.

Liquid gold, like rivulets of blood, seeps from the ground and crawls across my arms and chest. My skin blisters at its touch, waking white-hot agony. A scream shears free from the prison of my throat, soon smothered by the boiling liquid that fills my mouth and burns my tongue to cinders.

The sky spirit stops, her tears gleaming on the porcelain canvas of her face.

And those moonstone eyes—those doorways into her ageless soul—are the last thing I see before the mountain burns my eyes away too.

The gold-infused bones of the bone collector groan as I grind them between two boulders. The work is hard, and my fingers blister with the effort. My blood, clear as rain, wets my palms. But I do not falter.

My brother, Spirit of the Mountain, was kind and generous. When the universe cast me out alone to rule the skies, almost driven mad by that unending expanse, it was he that sang me back from oblivion. A gentle soul, he gave to the creatures that dwelt in his domain, and with their deaths, the power in their bones sustained him.

But the bone collector came. I watched from lofty heights as my brother's sustenance was stolen from him. I saw his body wilt as did the vegetation on the mountain—vegetation that he had, since the dawn of time, carefully cultivated.

And I wept when he died alone, his corpse left to rot on a mountainside turned fallow. Helplessness woke the rage of storms and wild winds in me.

And then the bone collector came again...

I push my weight down and grind the boulder harder. Bone shards splinter and spray across the snow. I carefully gather them back into the pile.

I grind.

I grind until all that is left is bone dust mixed

with gold. I carefully gather it up and move to stand at the precipice of the summit.

With pursed lips, I blow the particles into the air. The wind catches them, billows them across the sweeping dead forests that stretch below. As I stand with the morning sky arcing over me, I send a wish into the vastness of the universe. Please let it be that bones are not only bones but that they hold to deeper magic.

Let the bone collector's sacrifice return life to these lands.

NEW WORLD ORDER

A shirtless man trembles in the evening air, lips blue, his arms lashed to a post behind him. A plate-sized aluminium disc hangs around his neck. Painted red, the brush strokes are as thick and viscous as half-dried blood. This talisman, held close to the skin, is the first line of defence against those infected.

Infected because…this generation of humanity developed a taste for war.

Infected because…morality was sacrificed in the development of bio-engineered weaponry.

Infected because…

Truth is, the 'because' doesn't even matter anymore.

Private Howie Johns and Lieutenant David Brigham stand guard duty with me. Dressed in camo, their broad frames blur into the coming promise of night.

"I'm not sick," whines the bound man. "Let me go back inside."

Howie shifts on his feet. "You know we can't do that, John. Not yet. Twenty-four hours bound is the rule."

"But I've got a wife and child."

"That's why you're here. To make sure they stay safe."

Howie resumes his quiet stance, and I try to ignore the guilt prickling at me. I didn't become a soldier to treat civilians like this. This waiting to see *if* a person changes…in these moments, the victims are still lucid and they're scared, and I sure as hell don't blame them.

Minutes tick by. Dusk deepens. Soon the moon will rise and I cross my fingers hoping that when it does, this man is still a man.

"They need me…" whispers John.

David breaks. "Look, you weren't stung. A scratch like yours can go either way. There's still hope."

John slumps, weeping, against his bonds. I glance up. The moon crests the top of our defended court-yard's tall brick fence. For this moment, this one blessed moment, I think maybe he is okay and that we can take him home.

But then John's breaths grow rapid and sweat, at odds with the cold, suddenly slicks his brow. His lips curl and ripple as a growl builds in his throat. My heart sinks and I step back, my rifle positioned against my shoulder, finger set to the trigger.

"I...said...I'm not SICK!" John's words bubble with saliva and rage. His eyes snap open, sclera threaded through with red.

He bucks and his bonds cut deep against his wrists. He lunges forward, his shoulders knotted. The painted disc swings.

"He's done for!" yells Howie.

John howls, a sound to strip sanity. Past consideration for pain, he snaps his arms forward and his left shoulder dislocates, the bone pushing suddenly and unnervingly against taut skin. The bindings around his wrists snap and he leaps. Howie stumbles backward. His rifle barks, the bullet flying wide. The infected man's head tilts back and his mouth gapes. Something moves in the column of his throat—a saliva-coated insectoid leg, its end fitted with red-tipped stingers. It strikes, plunging into Howie's own neck, then retreats.

"Shit!" snarls Howie, clutching the wound.

Desperation strains his features. "I'm okay. I'm okay."

I fire—three bullets to end John's torment. The infected man straightens, rigid, eyes wide, and then slumps lifeless to the ground.

But this isn't over yet.

As Howie's curses fill the silence, the corpse shudders. The dead man's throat splits, torn flesh peeling outward, ragged and red. Something scaled bulges from the wound, something metallic green and black: a fledgling repax. The bloodied creature emerges with a hissing cry. It uncurls, its six articulated legs and elongated, reptilian abdomen consolidating into clean, slick lines. Its angular, armoured head lifts, mandibles clicking as it tastes the air.

I hate to admit it, but there is a certain beauty to the creature's design.

Like a newborn calf, the creature stumbles on its first step. In a rasp of scales and chitin, it collapses back into the ruin of John's corpse and against the aluminium disc. The parasite's connection to the painted metal initiates a chemical reaction. The disc begins to smoke and the paint, dosed heavily with cypermethrin, sizzles. The steam rises and surrounds the repax. It slows and stills—stunned.

David lights a match.

"Safe travels," he mutters, throwing it onto the creature.

Bullets, cypermethrin, and fire.

The only way to kill the parasitic monsters.

I retreat, holding my glove to my nose as the fire catches. John's corpse burns like torchwood, quick and bright, but the creature goes slower. The chemical drug wears off as it burns. I find no satisfaction in watching it suffer.

"Private!"

I hadn't even noticed David approach. "Tristan," he says, softer this time. "We need to help Howie."

"He was definitely stung?"

"Yeah."

I sigh, sorry for a pact made long ago and a promise I'll now need to keep.

Howie stands apart from us, rifle slung over one shoulder and his hands loose by his sides. He's a tall man—a brave soldier—a brother.

Howie turns, his hazel gaze resolute, his mouth twisted down into a grim line.

"I guess we all gotta go sometime," he says.

My stomach turns. I half lift my rifle, then drop it. That sting means he's infected for sure; I can't change that.

"Tristan," he whispers.

"I don't think I can do it, mate."

"Please." Howie's voice cracks. "I can't go back." He reaches up and touches the mark on his neck. "And I don't want one of those things growing in me."

I nod and lift the rifle.

"Tell Mollie I'm sorry," says Howie. "Tell her not to give up and that I love her."

Mollie. The strange little orphan girl he found and adopted. Hell, she'll be alone again now.

"I will." I bite my lip and steel myself. "Ready?"

Howie nods.

I don't look away as the trigger clicks.

I don't look away as the gun recoils.

And I don't look away as my friend falls to the ground, dead.

The correctional facility we occupy, with its high, razor-wired walls, is the most fortified building in town. Fifty-three men, women, and children shelter here, surviving off supplies pilfered from the abandoned city outside.

I secure my gun in the armoury racks and turn in. Falling to my bunk, the weight of grief crushes me, a blanket of sorrow and despondency. I swallow, still tasting the ash from the pyre.

I try and fail to recall what life used to be like—
the sound of civilisation, of barbecues with family in
parks and boat rides on the bay. I never saw this
miserable existence coming, but in retrospect, I
probably should have.

The president of the self-proclaimed 'New World
Order', after conquering all the nations of Europe,
turned his eye to the rest of the world. He warned
what would happen if all other nations refused to
kneel. *A fate worse than death*, he'd said. But then
Aussies have never taken well to being told what to
do. Our government told him to fuck off. We were
cocky—an island apart—a nation too far from the
main conflict to have real perspective on what was
to come. Only when the high-altitude drones blew
apart, seeding the rain clouds and our water sources
with parasitic eggs, did we learn the cost of defiance.

Footsteps draw my attention. I look up. Mollie,
nine years old, dressed in an oversized t-shirt and
holding her trademark fluffy pink toy, an octopus
named Kismet, stands in the doorway.

"Where's Howie?" she asks. "He isn't in his room."

I sit up and beckon her over. She trots closer and
climbs into my lap. Slight in the circle of my arms,
she's like a bundle of sticks held together with rubber
bands. She is such a solemn little girl—never one to

smile, never one to really play—it's almost like she isn't a child at all. Ever since Howie found her a year ago, wandering along the edge of the Brisbane River, it feels as if she has spent her time evaluating us.

"He didn't make it, Mol."

Her blue gaze remains steady. "Repax get him?"

"Yeah."

She tips her head to my shoulder. The loose strands of her chestnut hair tangle in the stubble of my beard. She smells of rainwater and something else—something peppery.

"Did they hurt him?"

Shame burns through me. I don't want to tell her how he died.

"No. Not Howie. He didn't feel any pain. He told me to tell you he was sorry, that he wanted you to keep going and that he loved you."

Mollie sits up; her small fingers weave through mine.

"It's best not to love anything too much, I think," she says. "Everyone dies."

I bite my lip. The bitterness in her breaks my heart. I wonder what this little girl endured before she came to us.

"You still have me, kid."

She glances up, eyes clear and hard. "For the

moment, but Howie was right. I've got to keep going."

"You're safe here, sweetheart. I think he meant he didn't want you to be sad."

"But I am sad. Howie was the only one who understood me."

I squeeze her hand and hold my tongue. I could offer platitudes, but she's too clever to believe them.

"Tristan, we're wanted." David appears from the corridor and leans against the door post. His uniform, like mine, is still dusted in ash and demoralisation. "General Jackson has something to show us."

"Okay." I touch Mollie's chin. "You head off, kiddo. I'll come find you afterwards."

The girl leaps off my lap and scuttles past David. He watches as she runs down the hall toward the dining room.

"You a new dad?" he asks.

"Looks like it."

General Jackson's office is sparse. A table, a wall-mounted pinboard covered in terrain maps, a laptop on his battered desk, and two chairs in front. Walnut hair, dark brown eyes, and unlined skin—he seems young for his station, but men twice his age lack the wicked smarts he possesses.

"You lost a friend today," he says, a statement rather than a question.

"Yes sir," I reply.

His jaw works as if he's trying to find the right words. "Don't beat yourself up. You did the right thing, Private."

I nod. Right or not, I still feel like shit.

Jackson looks away, as if considering the matter done. I guess he's got a point. Howie is past needing any more help.

"Engineering crew got a drone up this morning and they found something interesting."

The general swivels his laptop around. High-altitude surveillance footage plays on the screen. I recognise the hills behind the facility and the urban sprawl stretching to the horizon. The sunlight catches glints off the river that carves a serpentine path through the city centre.

The general flicks forward on the footage, stopping at the five-minute mark.

"Look here." He zooms the image in.

The nearby Westfield shopping centre's open-air plaza fills the screen. Except where greenery and pale terrazzo tiles once stretched, something dark now litters the scene. I squint and shapes formulate in the pixelated image. Long legs and scaled bodies lie tossed like limp spaghetti. Not one of the creatures moves.

"Fifteen adult repax, all dead, and it wasn't us," says Jackson. "I don't know how, but if we can work out what happened, we might be able to develop something to use as a weapon. Maybe we can turn the tide."

A fool's dream. I know better than to hope for anything other than survival. But then I recall Mollie's small, serious face. So young; her life barely lived at all. She deserves a chance to grow up—a chance to live in plenty.

"You need us to investigate." A statement of my own.

General Jackson nods.

The plaza is two kilometres away, but it may as well be fifteen. Close proximity sure as hell doesn't ensure our safety. David and I move quick and silent. Around us, the city looms oppressively, heavy with shadows and the funnelling of wind through the litter-filled alleyways. The sky is a strip of grey overhead, visible only in the space between the towering walls of empty skyscrapers. Rain hovers on the brink of falling, its weight bowing the clouds close.

"It's too quiet," mutters David.

I close up behind him, unable to shake the feeling of being watched.

"Next left and we're there," I say. "Keep your eyes open."

The plaza is quiet. Untrimmed greenery, planted when the world was a noisier place, spills from planter boxes. Rubbish, herded by years of weather, gathers in the doorways and corners.

Across the stained tiles sprawls a nest of repax, not long dead. Their jaws are stretched wide as if they'd died choking. I recoil at the look of their thick, forked tongues, lolled out across razored mandibles and covered in slick green excretions.

"Tristan, over here." David beckons from the opposite side of the courtyard. "Look."

I move closer. The largest of the repax, fully twelve feet long, lies at his feet. This one is in better condition than the others, but that isn't saying much. Weeping lesions cover the monster's body, inflamed and swollen around the wounds. Patches of scales have slid away, revealing the musculature beneath. I prod it with the end of my rifle.

The creature, not quite dead, recoils.

"Shit!" yells David.

He leaps clear, but I'm not so lucky. The repax rolls over, sluggish and heavy. One of its legs clips my heel. I pinwheel backward and slip over. My rifle skitters away and my sleeve brushes against the creature's leg.

A shot fires. The repax slumps heavily and doesn't move again.

"Are you all right?" yells David from behind his rifle's sight.

Urgent breaths make my lungs burn. My hands tremble as I pat myself over.

"I'm good."

"You sure?"

"Yes. No injury. All good."

David hunches over, breathing hard. He looks back up, features pale. "You're one lucky bastard. You know that right?"

"Yeah. I know." I swallow.

David approaches and cautiously circles the dead creature. He frowns.

"These things are diseased," he says. "I'll bet my pay cheque on it."

"We don't get paid. But I think you're right."

"The general might just have his answer," says David. "If we can weaponise whatever killed them…"

Falling rubble rattles by the doors leading into

the shops. I swivel on my heel. David holds up a hand, calling for silence.

The wind swirls leaves. He lowers his hand.

"Okay, let's head back. We'll get a couple of lads and a truck."

I'm more than ready to get out of here.

The rain begins to fall as we exit the plaza. Its cold touch seeps through the shoulders of my uniform and tracks an uncomfortable slide down my spine. The towering buildings, silent sentinels, mark our passage back toward the compound. We round a corner where three dead traffic lights stand guard over a broken street crossing. In the centre of the street lies sprawled a sodden, pink patch of colour. It takes me a moment to realise what it is.

A soft toy.

A pink octopus.

Kismet.

"Is that…?" David's words trail away.

I wipe the rain from my eyes and glance into the sleet. "Yep. Mollie's. She's out here." I curse myself. I should have made sure someone back at base was watching over her.

"If she is, she's in trouble," says David.

He's right. "You head back and get the truck," I say. "I'm going to find her."

"No," says David, "we both go back and get a crew to help."

I stride over and pick up the toy, brushing the water from its tentacles and leaf litter from the bulbous head. "She's out here because of me. We can't waste time."

David's mouth presses thin. "That thing killed Howie, not you."

"I pulled the trigger."

"Tristan…"

"Go. I'm not leaving her."

David's hands clench. Outranking me he can order my compliance, but as a friend he knows how important this is to me. He fumbles at the clip on his belt and hands me two grenades.

"I'll meet you back at the compound. Good luck."

I follow the road that leads toward the river. Kismet, secured at my belt, bounces against my thigh at each step. I keep a keen eye on the shadowed places I pass.

The river, riding easy at the top of the tide, appears from between the old casino and the city library building. A cry echoes out to my left and I turn. It's a gull taking to the air, water dripping from its feet.

And then I see a small, white figure crouched in the mud by the water's edge. Her chestnut hair, slicked to her skull, is a smudge of warmth against the pallor of the day.

"Mollie!"

She surges upright, holding her hands hidden behind her. The front of her shirt is streaked with mud.

"Come to me," I say.

She bites her lip and glances around her. Why is she hesitating?

"Quickly."

"You don't need to be afraid, Tristan," she says, her small voice carrying well. "Nothing here will hurt you."

I juggle my rifle against my shoulder and glance toward the water. Nothing moves.

"Mollie, it's dangerous out here. We need to get back." I unclip Kismet from my belt and hold him out. Water trails from my fingers and from the sodden toy's tentacles. "C'mon, Kismet's scared. Let's get him back to safety."

She glances at the toy but makes no move to take it. Her gaze fixes to mine.

"You're so quick to kill them," she says, her small voice tight. "You don't even know the truth."

"What are you talking about?"

"What was done to them was evil."

"Mollie?"

The little girl's chin lifts. "Spider wasps, rough-scaled snakes, and moray eels. That's what the repax were before they mixed them all together."

"Mixed them?"

"The genetic parts that make them, them."

I frown. The girl's stance has shifted. Mollie then turns and faces the water. The river ripples, the coffee-brown water swelling and agitating. The surface breaks into a line of long, dark, metallic backs curving upward.

I let the toy fall. My grip resets around my rifle. "Mollie, get back here."

"No, you need to see what comes next."

The little girl kneels as a nest of repax, twelve strong, exit the water and climb the bank to gather around her. Their bodies gleam wetly in the grey light, and a thrumming buzz emanates from their terrible mouths.

Mollie's voice lowers to a whisper. "They're corrupted, Tristan, and they're in pain. It's wrong to let them suffer."

The creatures rise on their articulated legs, exposing their muscular underbellies to the little girl. Only now do I notice the raw lesions covering them, the patches of scales slanted askew—putrefied and slipping from their bodies.

"The water is full of filth—polluted," says Mollie. "They have nowhere else to go. Humans made them and now leave them diseased and dying."

"That's a good thing, Mol."

Mollie's small face hardens. "Howie knew the truth."

Her words make no sense, but either does seeing her surrounded by docile repax. I've only ever known them to be brutal in their singular purpose: their drive to reproduce.

I juggle the gun in my sweaty palms.

"What did Howie know?"

Mollie places a hand on the closest of the beasts. It straightens and then slumps forward. Its mouth opens as it tries to breathe, long tongue lashing against its teeth. It hisses once and then falls still. Green bile floods from its open, distended maw.

The other repax remain still.

"He knew I was the solution," says Mollie. "He knew I was another mutant—bacteria bred into human form and sent here by the New World Order to kill repax. They believe you've been exterminated and now want your country cleared for repopulation." She glances around. "But Howie taught me to think differently. You shouldn't be made to surrender your homes."

"So, you killed the repax in the plaza for us?"

"Yes. And there are more still out there. Let me continue to do my work, as Howie did."

"But the others won't let you back in if you don't come with me now."

She tilts her head and blinks. The rain has eased to a sprinkle. Water beads on her eyelashes.

"They won't let either of us in, Tristan," she says, "even if we do go back."

Mollie moves closer, looking so small. She gently touches her hand to my rifle and, compelled, I lower it. She gathers my right hand into hers and opens my palm.

My breath catches. I missed the injury back in the plaza. She runs a gentle thumb over a shallow scratch that crosses my palm and glances up at me. "I can smell it in your blood. I'm sorry."

"Smell what?" But I already suspect the answer. My heart thunders against my ribs, and the rain running down my spine suddenly feels more like sweat than water.

Mollie retrieves Kismet and hugs him to her chest.

"The repax growing in you."

I bite my lip and taste blood. A thousand

thoughts race, but the loudest is that I'm here alone. No Howie to keep a promise. No David to let the others know what happened. Sorrow, grief, and anger are consuming.

But Mollie is here. She doesn't need to see me fall apart; she needs me to be the best example of humanity I can be.

I let go of the breath I've been holding and kneel down to Mollie's level. I find the strength to smile, even though all I want to do is scream.

"You should go and do your work."

"What about you?"

Words fail me but she doesn't seem to need them. Maybe Howie told her about the pact.

Mollie nods and gently hugs me, then presses Kismet into my hand.

"He'll help you," she says, glancing back at the repax still waiting on the riverbank. "And they won't hurt you. I've told them to wait."

I grasp the toy tightly and smile. "Thank you."

Mollie nods and walks away, headed toward the empty city. I watch her go and too soon, her small form disappears around a street corner. I wait another minute just to make sure she's safe. I turn and approach the gathered repax. They don't move, sitting and waiting just as they have been told to.

I tuck Kismet into my belt, unclip the two grenades David gave me, and release the pins.

"I guess we all gotta go sometime," I whisper.

A MOTHER'S SON

11 November, 1916

It begins with a bright blue sky over Sydney Harbour. The sound of waves lapping against the hull of the giant troopship, and you standing off to one side of the swirling crowd of onlookers who wave us goodbye. Mum, you look so tall and so still amongst that surging sea of humanity, your lips pressed thin and eyes glittering with disapproval. You don't want me to go, but I refuse to be left behind.

The boatswain's whistle sounds, and the great anchor chain rattles. The troopship HMAT *Suevic* groans as her steam engines wake the great blades of her motors. Her angled bow leans out from the dock as she readies to leave the harbour. The crowd below roars, an upwelling of colour and jubilation, and the soldiers around me respond in kind, waving enthusiastically as they lean over the rails to bid their own farewells.

My heart is carried high on the cresting tide of anticipation, because this all feels like such a great adventure.

It's only a moment more before you dwindle into the distance. Mum, you are so pale in contrast to the crisp colours of the Australian flags fluttering amongst the crowd. You somehow make the pomp and celebration seem unreal, ghostly, in contrast to your desperate reality. Such sorrow weighs in those dark eyes of yours; eyes that have loved and watched over me since the day I was born. I know you fear I'll not return.

Your only son, your only child. I was and remain your world.

I raise my hand. Not a farewell but a promise to stay safe. I must go, Mum. I am nineteen, and the shores of France and Belgium are calling for all of us Aussie lads to bear arms. I go to protect the world you brought me into.

---

21 December, 1916

The most surprising thing about England is the colour of the sky. It's different from home. In Inverell, the skies are a vibrant blue—the kind of blue that has a three-dimensional depth to it—but here it's more watercolour-pale, hard and grey like the colour of ice.

I've made it to Larkhill camp and am being trained to fight on a Lewis gun. The accommodations are bleak, and the chalk-lined roads are sticky in the wet. The sunnier days are even worse, with the dust raised from those same roads so fine as to choke a man. The nights spent sleeping on hard boards in our tin huts give no respite. Mud, dust and frozen feet; days rendered repetitive by the endless drills and commands—'Stand at ease', 'Slope arms', 'Quick march', 'Attention', 'Fix bayonets'.

I'm thankful though, because it means I can keep my promise to you. I take care to pay attention and learn the lessons well.

It's said that the life expectancy of a gunner is only ten hours of firing time.

For your sake, Mum, I will do better than that.

29 March, 1917

Fourteen weeks of training across Christmas has led us into England's spring. New Year's Eve was as raucous an affair as could be mustered in the camp. No women here, but the extra rations of bacon and cheese were wonderful. Rum was handed out, and the younger lads who had never known much about drinking partook to excess. I saw you lingering in the doorway as I led the singing; that lovely chorus of 'Waltzing Matilda' got many lads up on their feet, boots stomping on the timber floor of the corrugated iron-walled bar.

But we have received our marching orders today. We are headed for France. I'm eager to escape the tedium of these last months. As a battalion, we are united, trained and ready to fight.

As I strap my pack, a young lieutenant has appeared from around the side of our hut. Gold braid glints on his left sleeve—three wound stripes—he's seen action. He looks lost.

"Are you all right, sir?"

The officer turns at my words; his eyes haunted and hard, shoulders held with brittle-glass tension. My breath hitches. His face is a mask of ruin; the gunshot scar across his cheek, an angry, dark and gnarled thing that twists his top lip into a bitter knot.

"I seem to have been turned around," he says. "I'm looking for the officer's quarters."

"Left at the next crossing, sir," I reply, voice lowered.

He nods. His boots wake dust as he passes.

Mum, did you lead this man astray so I could see? Do you mean to scare me?

It's too late to change my mind. The trucks are already rolling in through the front gate to take us to the station at Amesbury. I'm ready to do my bit.

As the first strains of the 'Colonel Bogie March' rise from the battalion band, I adjust my slouch hat and check my kit one last time. I look around.

Mum, I see you standing by the gate. Please stop crying, for your sake and mine.

These lads I stand with are strong and willing and brave. We are the pride of Australia. You have nothing to fear.

---

5 July, 1917

I have forgotten what the sky at home looks like.

I can't recall the scent of clean air or the taste of home-cooked food. A fetid pall hangs over everything in this god-forsaken place.

We can't get to our dead in no man's land, and they have been left to lie where they fell. The stench is barely covered by the aroma of the tobacco we smoke in the moments between the chaos of war. I am one of the last few remaining of those who left Larkhill that day so many months ago. I see you, Mum, standing at the end of the trench, your face hidden in your hands. At least I've made it past the typical ten hours, but I'm no longer sure I'll make it home. I'll try, but I am sorry if all your effort into raising me right amounts to nothing.

I am glad you are here with me, though. I lean into the wall of the trench, tucked up close with my coat around me. The atmosphere is thick with the ghosts of the already fallen and the thoughts of those fearing what is to come. Some of the men are writing in their journals, others sit quietly as they wait for the sky to lighten into morning. Here in the pre-dawn, I feel hollowed out and empty. I try to recall the safety I once felt in the circle of your arms when, as a child, I feared monsters. But that protection is only a memory, and the monsters here at the Western Front are not the kind found hiding under beds.

"You got a cigarette?"

A private watches me from the opposite side of the trench. His face is like so many others here, a young canvas with eyes that seem too old. He smiles, grim yet hopeful that the simple pleasure can be granted.

What a soldier has, he willingly gives. I reach into my top pocket and hand my packet to him. He takes one and hands it back. His features illuminate suddenly in the flare born as he strikes a match.

"Thanks."

I nod and curl in deeper against the wall. I close my eyes to try and snatch a few moments of sleep. It's quiet for the moment, but everyone is on edge. Pray for me, mum. We go 'over the top' again soon.

6 July, 1917

Fear fades in the moment I leap over the edge. There is only the whine of bullets by my ear and the hope that if the end comes, it will be quick. I keep low as I run. Cobber John Davies, my loader on the Lewis, fell ten meters back and, unable to carry the gun alone, I left it with him. I've taken a rifle from a fallen man.

I reach a hole and tumble in, falling short against something soft and unmoving. I turn and wipe the mud from my eyes. The young private from the night before lies there, slouch hat askew, face still and dark eyes tilted to the dawn sky. As bullets pepper the rim, I duck. Mum, you are kneeling in the mud next to me. I only stay long enough to see you close the boy's eyes and mutter a prayer over him.

The men are scattered, lost amongst clouds of artillery smoke and the shrapnel-filled columns of dirt exploding skyward. I don't know how I've made it so far, but suddenly there is a line of wire ahead. I leap over it, joined by three others, brothers-in-arms, identities hidden behind the filth of battle. Together we fall into the first of the enemy's trenches, and the gunshots quieten into the more intimate brutality of killing with the bayonet.

Mum, I hate that I must look them in the eye while doing this. Killing from afar is far easier than doing it while smelling a man's sweat and feeling his desperate breaths on your skin. I hate that feeling as the knife slides in and the hot rush of blood that follows. But I feel your hand on my shoulder, steadying me. I see the fire in your eyes as they come for me, and how your teeth are bared against them. I'm sorry I brought you here, Mum. I am so sorry.

The next man to climb over his dead predecessor is quick. His bayonet drips red, and his snarl is like a dingo's. His mother stands by his shoulder too, small and fiery. Her eyes are like England's skies—grey and hard as ice. She walks with her boy, willing him to return home also. Mum, I see you settle into your fighting stance. I'll take the son if you can watch the woman.

The next few moments are fluid. Smoke and mud and noise, I lunge for the man but miss. A sudden sting and the crunch of bone in my shoulder cripples as the enemy's blade pierces deep. I scream as he twists the metal, and my arm drops, useless. I slip to my knees and cry out again, this time furious, as I drive my wounded shoulder into the man's thigh. He stumbles but doesn't fall. Then he grins, teeth white, as he realises my rifle lies discarded in the mud. He jerks up his arms, bayonet poised.

Mum, do you sense my death as clearly as I do?

---

7 July, 1917

The canvas walls of the clearing station ripple softly in the breeze. Clean white bandages wrap my wound. I don't remember being brought in.

A young, dark-haired medic moves amongst the beds, tending to the wounded men lying upon them.

His once-white apron is patched and stained; the memory of other men's blood held in the weave.

"You're awake, cobber. Good to see." His voice is calm—an island in contrast to the battlefield roar still ringing in my ears.

"How did I get here?" I ask.

He glances across at me and then away. "Bearers brought you in. They said it was the damnedest thing. You were found in the front-line trench under a dead German. The man didn't have a mark on him."

I feel the mattress settle as you sit on the end of my bed. You saved me, didn't you, Mum? I imagine you reached in and crushed that man's heart.

"You were lucky to make it out of that mess." The medic checks my bindings with slim hands that smell of antiseptic. "So many other blokes didn't. Now it'll be back to England for you to heal, and then home, I'd say. With this injury, you won't be lifting anything again."

The medic gently taps my arm. "You got anyone at home waiting for you?"

"No," I reply. "Just a farm to tend."

"What? Not even a mother who'll be glad to have her boy back?"

"No. There's no one left at home."

TENEBROUS

I favour the flipvoid over real space. That non-place of existence between planets. It reminds me of the oceans of my home world, Aquanum. Only darker. A plane of endless black: a plane where monsters roam. And it's also where my elusive nightmare lingers. A nightmare as real as breathing. One I've searched long years to find and to kill.

Still the hunt goes on.

"Fishin' grounds ahead, Zesa," I call over my shoulder. "Better haul that arse of yours and get the customers sorted."

The ship's viewscreen reflects the cabin and the movements of my first mate behind me. Zesa rises from her seat at the far end of the cockpit. Her short hair glints copper in the bright cabin lights. Her neck, translucent white, gleams like marble against the polished black collar of her armoured voidsuit. She taps a button on the navicomp control, transferring radar output to my console.

"Of course, Tiswin," she says. "But only because you asked so nicely."

I shrug. "Nice is for nursefish, not captains."

"You're not a real Hegemon captain. You still know that, right?"

I tap the faded insignia on my jacket—a jacket I found abandoned in a bar on a station in the Glondian system. "That ain't what the badge says, sister."

Zesa rolls her eyes. "That's not your badge."

"Hegemon ain't got no authority here in the flipvoid. That means I'm the bossman and the badge confirms it."

Zesa's lips pinch together. Her yellow eyes narrow, but there's laughter in her gaze. She dips her chin to glance out the ship's viewscreen. The display panel shows the void. A sea of shadows, darkness shifting and roiling.

She frowns. "Currents look strong out there. You alright to keep us steady on your own?"

I grin a debonair smile and wiggle my facial tentacles. "Me? Come on. I eat void currents for breakfast."

Zesa chuckles, the sound rich like warm chocolate. 'I've seen what you eat for breakfast. Space eel à la carte isn't nearly as dangerous.'

"You've never tried eating the space eel alive."

"And I thank the Creator for that." She flips a sarcastic salute. "I'm off. Call me if you need anything."

The cockpit door leading to the cargo bay unseals and opens. Zesa exits, her voice echoing off the metal corridor as she calls the passengers up.

"You can unclip your travel harnesses. Voidsuits are in the lockers. Those of you without aural implants will find your translator and comms earbud in the top pockets. Let me know if you need help fitting them."

Her voice fades as the door closes and re-seals. The cabin grows colder and quieter without her. Just the tiny, regular beeps of the radar scanner keep me company. It's too quiet. I hate the quiet. It brings memories.

First the slow, familiar slither of pain crawling across my chest—a chest half prosthetic, since the day one of my three hearts was torn out. The sensation is in my mind, not real. But even now, after ten long years, the phantom pains afflict me.

And then the waking nightmares. Such nightmares. The visions borne of darkness and teeth and eyes like red coals. In their thrall I taste my blood. My far-left heart is again ripped away and the haunting call of my nemesis holds me teetering on the edge of sanity. No one else knows of the visions. If they did, I would be diagnosed with flip psychosis and locked away. But it's not that. I'm perfectly sane. I just need to find and kill the creature that crippled me.

Find it.

Kill it.

Then the memory of the blood I taste won't be mine anymore.

And the nightmares will no longer eat me.

I take a shuddering breath, thinking of Zesa to try and thaw the ice crawling down my spine. She's my first mate, but also my anchor. A Yoobrillian biologist here cataloguing void creatures, she found me floating in space all those years ago. She gathered up my shattered body and patched it to save my life. And, when I told my story, she believed me. Maybe it was something to do with the logician in her Yoobrillian nature. But she's been by my side ever since, supporting my quest.

My friend. My conscience.

My tie to reality.

I glance at the radar scanner. Blue pulses of light circle out from the centre, showing nothing more sinister than a small makovoid swarm huddled a klick to port. No creatures the size of small moons lurk here. I growl, hating myself for fearing what I come here every trip to kill. And that which I fail to find.

The Tenebrous.

The memory of it rises before me. Blue and silver skin and rows of wicked teeth stacked like knives. The single kill spot on the roof of its mouth. I press back into my chair, my palms tingling. My breaths come short and sharp.

Then my aural implant buzzes in my ear.

Zesa's voice crackles over the comms. "We are suited up in here, Tis."

I blink, and the hallucination fades but my hearts still beat an uneasy tattoo. I take a deep breath and collect myself.

"Good one," I reply. "Hang a bit. I'll anchor up."

"Right-o."

The lever next to the control wheel slides down in one slick movement. The viewscreen displays the anchor parachutes as they flare out, one from each side of the ship. Two great sheets of treated rhodium, beaten to a shining foil, bell out and gather the flipdrive's excess particles to hold us in place. The surface of each chute, illuminated by its own anchor light, undulates in the void current, beautiful like molten mercury.

"Cargo bay opening," I confirm.

"Aye. Good to go," says Zesa.

The escaping atmosphere hisses behind the closed cockpit door. A light blinks red on the console. *Atmosphere purge complete.* The radar screen beeps, changing to register dots aft of the ship. Zesa and our three customers. Four fishers all up. I close the cargo doors, re-pressurise the bay, and then shift the viewscreen display. Zesa, dressed in her black suit, is only visible by the blue illumination of her helmet. The others, a Dirty from Earth, an Iscean, and a Kronck are all in white voidsuits. They bob like moths against the dark. Each customer is armed with an electro-rod—a slender, red spear that can be used to stun a makovoid at fifty paces.

"Can you give us a heading on the school?" crackles Zesa over the comms.

I glance back at the radar. "Thirty metres to port. Careful of the currents."

"Listen, everybody," says Zesa, addressing the customers. "We need to move quietly or we'll miss. Rear suit thrustors are used for forward propulsion. Short bursts and let the momentum carry you before you use it again. Hand thrustors are only for course corrections. Everyone understand?"

Agreement in three different languages scratches through my ear implant. No translation. I tap it. If

I'm lucky, it's usually only the translator function that's finicky; other times the whole unit fails. The damn thing needs to be replaced.

It clicks and the implant comes back online. The Kronck is speaking. One type of alien species you do not want to piss off.

"You conssssider this sssssneaking up to be hunting?" lisps its insectoid voice. "There is no honour in thisss. It issss not how Kroncks hunt. The kill must be made face to face. I want to ssssee the makovoid's eyes when it diessss."

I smile. Customers like this one are why Zesa oversees public relations. My tendency toward a "sit down and shut up" methodology isn't always the best way to deal with some aliens.

"This is the only way to capture this type of creature," says Zesa carefully. "They're quick, smart, and extremely flighty. But, if you will follow my direction closely, none of us will go home empty handed."

The male Dirty, too stupid for his own good, sniggers. The Kronck growls in return.

But the Iscean steps in. "Our host is correct. Makovoids are capricious. Let us put aside our egos and get to fishing shall we, gentlemen?" she says. "I'm sure we are all looking forward to a fine feast tonight."

The Kronck grunts, the sound untranslatable, but nothing more is said.

The group, stretched out in a line, follows Zesa past the ship. I track their progress on the radar. Twenty-five meters. Fifteen meters. They are right on the school. I look back to the viewscreen.

Electricity, shaped like lightning, bristles against the darkness. The four fishers are silhouetted against the brightness. Black cardboard cut-outs. My comms blink alert, a cacophony of voices screeching against my eardrum. Something about the Kronck shooting too soon. Something about Zesa being hit.

I duck as the school of makovoid shoots past the ship. Tentacles streaming out behind them, their bullet-nosed, sapphire bodies glint for a moment in the ship's anchor lights. Then they're gone.

But the noise is still raging in my ear. Something has gone terribly wrong out there.

"Zesa? What's goin' on, darlin'?"

No answer.

But the Iscean's voice bursts suddenly into my ear, sharp as a knife. "Pilot, your female has been hit. Her suit is damaged…" A pause. "Oxygen convertors are destroyed. We won't get her back to you in time. Can you bring the ship to us?"

I slam the console. "Fecking hell," I snarl. I can't release the anchors. If I do, the ship will fall back into normal space, leaving the lot of them stranded in the void. Only one choice here. "Can't do. But hold on to her. I'll come out to you."

I do three things at once. One tentacle presses the auto-pilot. One repressurises the cargo bay, and another transfers the radar read to my ocular implant. The blue lines bloom before my right eye in concentric circles; the four dots representing those outside are pinpoints of light against my retina.

Zesa.

I can't lose her.

I race into the cargo bay. Two white voidsuits remain in the lockers. Neither fully charged. I scramble into one. I curl my tentacles into the collar and slip the helmet on. The other voidsuit I tie around my arm.

I pull the manual release lever for the cargo bay doors. The atmosphere explodes from the airlock, pushing me clear of the ship. I engage the suit thrustors and angle my way toward the cluster of helmet lights. I travel fast, but not fast enough. Every second wasted is a moment less for Zesa.

I growl as the low power alarm blares across my helmet's screen. Dammit. The void currents are too strong, just keeping on course has depleted the first of the power cells. But there should still be enough charge to get me to Zesa and back.

The cluster of lights grows brighter. The view grows clearer. The limp form of my first mate floats gently in the centre of the huddle. I swallow my desperation.

I'm travelling too fast. My momentum carries me into the circle of customers and scatters them like leaves. As I pass, I catch Zesa around the waist. Her inertia anchors me. Another burst from my back-pack does the rest to help me stop.

Hanging in the velvet darkness, I turn her toward me. The right arm casing of her voidsuit crumples under my touch. The oxygen compartment has been breached. The canisters are all gone.

Zesa's face comes into view, bloodied, behind the crack in her visor. Her lips are dark blue, her eyelids flutter and jerk.

Panic swells in my chest. My prosthetic heart shivers, beating out of alignment with the other two. My ID implant activates, registering the high level of stress on my biorhythms. I blink and the readout switches to Zesa's status.

Transferred patient status: Onset of critical hypoxia. Pulmonary hypertension.

"By the fecking Creator," I snarl. "Someone come and help me."

I turn and find the Iscean female already floating next to me.

"Here, hold her." I push Zesa into the reptilian woman's arms. She holds her while I undo the spare void suit from my arm and crack open the unit's sleeve covering. Inside rests the small oxygen generator's canister. I tear it free; the thin wires connecting it to the suit twist and snap.

"This is gonna be a real patch job, darlin'," I mutter to Zesa's inert form.

The broken top layer of Zesa's sleeve peels back like an eggshell. The stripped wires, where the original canisters were, gleam bright. Quickly, I twist the wire ends together, cursing the awkwardness of my gloves, and then shove the unit back into the compartment.

Zesa sucks in a breath as oxygen floods her suit. Her eyes snap open; their bright yellow hue is a sharp contrast to her violet-coloured, half-human, half-Yoobrillian blood.

The Iscean lets go of Zesa. The comms light on the woman's earbud blinks on. "The helmet is still cracked. We need to get her back before it ruptures."

"Aye," I say. "Collect up the others. We're done fishin' for today."

The Kronck hangs back, strangely silent on the return trip to the ship. It's like he knows that every part of me wants to tear the exoskeleton off his back for what he did. But Zesa has forbidden it.

"Let it go," she says yet again to me on the private comms channel. "It was an honest mistake. The Kronck accidently released the safety on the rod. I went in to fix it and it discharged."

"Or he pulled the trigger. You know, wanting better prey than a makovoid."

"Kroncks are rude bastards, but honourable. It was a mistake, I'm sure of it."

I let the matter drop but the anger still bubbles inside of me. I'm sick of this gig, sick of dealing with ungrateful, useless customers. Especially this whingeing lot. I have a sudden urge to get back on board and drop all of them off at the nearest aster-oid. Let them rot there.

But Zesa won't allow it. She'd say we need the credits they owe us.

And she's right. No credits means a trip to the Underground Banker and a visit to that loan shark is never a good idea.

I glance at the radar display again on my helmet visor. The makovoid swarms have all fled. This section of flipvoid is now empty except for the ship and us.

But the ship's mark—it's bigger than it should be. Almost the size of a small moon.

I look back at the ship. Its bulbous lines are clearly visible in the glow of the anchor lights—a beetle pinned against velvet. For a moment, everything is still except for faint ripples in the darkness around the ship caused by the active flipdrive. But then the ripples start to grow. Wider and wider, they crease the darkness into ominous waves. Small to large. Large to tidal.

Then something else is illuminated: a mountain of flesh, silver, and undulating blue traced through with a line of jagged, brilliant white. A huge head materialises, a maw bristling with a wall of wicked teeth.

The mouth opens wider.

And then the ship, anchor parachutes and all, is inhaled into the monstrous mouth.

"What the feck is that?" yells the Dirty.

My palms turn to sweat. My stomach rolls. But not because our only way back to real space has been taken, but because I finally have a chance for revenge.

I smile, my tentacles tingling. "That's the fecking tenebrous."

Without the lights of the ship to hide it, the pale, quavering red light emanating from the edges of the tenebrous' fins is revealed, watercolour scarlet against the infinite black. Then the glow fades and darkness falls to shroud the monster. It's still there, but hunting; veiled. I imagine the thud of its heartbeat around me.

I let go of Zesa. "Give me an electro-rod."

"Tiswin, *no!*" says Zesa. "Don't be crazy. You can't go after it by yourself."

A rod is pressed into my hand. It's the Kronck, handing me Zesa's abandoned spear. His eyes glitter in the light from his helmet.

"He doessss not go alone," he says to Zesa. "My kind have hunted the tenebroussss for centuriessss. Few ever return. But when they do, they come with tales of an inssssatiable creature that never sssstops until everything is consumed—machine and flesh alike. But to kill it gives ussss a chance to ssssurvive. The creature's carcassss will regisssster on a sensor. Another sssship travelling through flip will ssssstop to invessssstigate. They can take us back to real sssspace."

Zesa's gaze is like a brand as she watches me take the rod. She knows me too well; knows that while the Kronck is right, that is not why I want to fight. I have waited ten years for revenge. Now is my time.

"I will fight alongsssside you," says the Kronck, nodding. "Live or die, thissss is an honourable hunt."

"Count me in," says the Dirty. "That thing's nothin' more than a great big space shark, and I'm considered the best shark fisherman on Earth. I got your back."

I'm not sure that Earth's shark species are even comparable to what we face, but the human will be good bait if nothing else.

The Iscean stays with Zesa. The Dirty and the Kronck fan out around me.

We wait.

We wait.

The light of the tenebrous swells to life on our left. The tip of my electro-rod blares active-white. The other two follow. I press the suit's thrustors and sail toward my quarry.

Zesa's voice crackles in my ear. "Come back alive, Tis."

"No fear, darlin'," I reply. "I'll get ya home."

"It's *you* not coming home I'm worried about."

I've no chance to answer. The tenebrous roars, a silent wall of pressure carried through the void. I increase the force of my suit's thrustors, and sail through the disturbed current unaffected. And so does the Kronck. But the Dirty wobbles. He tumbles, shunted off course, before readjusting and falling back into place behind us. The power cell alarm beeps again in my helmet. My second power cell is depleted.

Only one to go. It'll have to be enough.

The tenebrous rises as a wall of flesh before us. Its mouth, the size of a battle cruiser, hangs open sucking in the void current. I am drawn forward. Closer and closer to that bone-lined opening. Closer to the animal's single kill-spot.

I press the trigger on the electro-rod. It burgeons to life. A spider web of electricity crackles out, encasing half of the beast's face. The rest is covered as the Kronck's and the Dirty's weapons activate. The tenebrous rears and slews sideways as it tries to free its head from the expanding web of power.

The creature lunges forward. It breaks free and draws in a mighty breath. I roll to the side, aided by the quick press of my hand thrustor. But the Dirty is caught in the flow. He screams as he is pulled into the cavernous mouth. Panicked, he activates his electro-rod again.

But he is too late. His weapon is sucked along with him down the tenebrous' throat.

The Kronck appears by my side. "Aim for the eyessss!" he screams into his comms bud. "Blind it!"

I aim my weapon. Electricity blurs to life again. I

fire. The Kronck's beam joins mine to fall on the tenebrous' left eye.

The orb of flesh, the softest part of the creature, disintegrates. A clouding mist of yellow blood stains the backdrop of flipspace. The tenebrous shrieks and I smile, teeth bared.

"Take that, you bastard," I mutter.

The creature rolls away. The pale expanse of its belly is momentarily revealed, pink against the glow of its internal light. Then the light fades.

Silence falls.

The Kronck floats in close. "My suit issss almost out of power," he says.

"Mine too. We need to end this soon. Inside its mouth is the way to kill it."

I look at him. The metallic-looking matrix of his insectoid eyes glitters. He grins at me.

"We can do thisss," he says.

I like the Kronck. He's an alien after my own hearts.

The tenebrous' light awakens again overhead. Yellow ichor trails from its damaged eye.

"Follow me!" yells the Kronck as he shoots forward. His momentum carries him to the open wound. He rears back and jams the activated electro-rod into the creature's damaged eye.

The tenebrous bucks. The Kronck, still grasping

the electro-rod, is flung against the side of the animal. Then the creature drops its great fluke, a fin ridged with sharpened bone and glittering points of red light. It catches the Kronck.

His suit fractures.

My translator crackles to life. The Kronck is laughing.

"An honourable death," he says.

Then his body, the exoskeleton now revealed, cracks apart like an eggshell. The shattered remains float away, scattered by the void's current.

I grip the smooth edge of my electro-rod. Rage and sorrow war within me, but my resolve is iron hard.

Zesa's voice sounds small in my ear. "Please come back," she says. "Let it go, Tis. It's not worth your life. Don't leave me here without you."

"I'll always be with you, darlin'," I say. "Now be brave. I gotta see you girls get home."

I sail forward with my suit's power alarm ringing in my ears. I am focused, my hearts beating a slow, steady rhythm. I am ready. I just need to get the timing right.

The tenebrous' mouth opens, a red, light-lined cavern. My suit's thrustors shudder and then, with a final burst, hiss to a stop. The alarm cuts off mid-beep. The suit's automated voice activates.

Power shutdown. Three minutes of oxygen remaining.

It'll be enough.

It has to be enough.

The creature inhales again, pulling me deeper into its maw. I sail past the first of ten rows of teeth and down toward the darkness of its throat. I activate my electro-rod and look up. I watch and wait. Wait for the moment. Wait for the spot I saw ten years ago, just past the last ridge of teeth at the top of its mouth. Back then I accidently punched it—that small patch of tender flesh. It was enough for the creature to spit me out.

But today, I am properly armed.

The dark spot of flesh crosses my vision. The size of a melon.

I aim the electro-rod, press the trigger, and pour electricity into the beast.

Death is instantaneous. The tenebrous plunges into a nose-dive and a gush of yellow blood waterfalls over me. I lose my grip on the rod. I spiral, blinded, in space. I hit hard flesh. I scrape over razor teeth.

Then silence.

Power shutdown. Oxygen. Thirty seconds remaining.

Spiral. Spiral. Spiral.

I can't see anything past the blood on my visor.

Twenty seconds remaining.

My breath thunders in my ears.

At least the tenebrous is dead.

I can rest easy in that knowledge.

My momentum slows. Hands pull at me. Gloved fingers scrape across my suit visor, smearing away the tenebrous' blood. Zesa's face appears, her lovely eyes wide. Her lips are stretched to thin lines. She is screaming at me. But the words don't reach me. My fickle comms has failed me.

But I don't need to hear her. I already know what she is saying. And I wish she could save me too. But there is nothing we can do. I'm already breathing fumes.

Ten seconds remaining.

My gaze moves past Zesa's face, drawn by a distant glow. I bark out a choking laugh, delighted by what I see. In the distance hover the illuminated parachute anchors of a Hegemon cargo hauler.

Salvation.

For the girls at least.

Zesa and the Iscean will make it home.

It's harder to breathe. My throat works to suck in air that just isn't there. Only seconds left now. Shuttles ease away from the hauler, coming for us, but their progress is slow against the void-current. I'll be dead by the time they get to us. So close, but so far.

I look back at Zesa. Beautiful, loyal Zesa. I blink and press a tentacle against the inside of my visor. Her fingers line up with my touch.

"Goodbye, darlin'," I whisper.

Oxygen depleted.

Zesa's face crumples with grief. But she holds my gaze as I fight my final choking breaths.

She holds my gaze until I fail, until the darkness creeps in.

The last thing I see are her tears falling.

DESERT GODS

A curse on the gold
Riches steeped in greed.
Held in a dead man's skull
Demanding retribution.

A harsh sun rises over peaks and winding canyons, their lengths dotted with stretches of desert ironwood, and creosote bush. The air harbours the chill of night, but it flees quickly, replaced by the rising scent of warming stone and wiry grasses. But any beauty is wasted on me. No matter how far or how fast I've run, how much I wish I could deny what lies behind, the memory of a dead man follows me.

Shadows flitter in my periphery. Memories of the

previous night set against a moonlit desert. The image of Tate's hand outstretched and his voice demanding—

"Don't you dare, Brody!"

Guilt surges, acid and biting. Its touch builds a different kind of desert in my throat.

Disembodied whispers carry on the breeze. I'm not sure if they're born of my own burdened conscience or of others lost to this wild place. Unseen fingers brush against my lips and pluck at my shirt. The wind sighs as if it holds the power to speak—

I saw you...

I spin, a burning breath held in lungs that ache for release. I narrow my gaze against the morning, the brilliance of its red-yellow light that casts dewdrops into diamonds and every other detail into sharp relief. There is only the rising chorus of waking cicadas.

But there are eyes on me, I swear it.

I resume my staggering trot toward the jagged horizon. I have no specific destination in mind, knowing only that I must get *away*—away from what I have done.

"Don't you dare, Brody!"

I glance across my shoulder, breath hissing between clenched teeth. I twist trembling fingers into the corded tie of the satchel hanging at my belt. The weight of the gold nugget within presses against my leg.

But there's no comfort in its presence.

Only bitter denunciation.

Do not dig us from land
Already drenched in blood.
To unearth by force
Invites torment.

We worked during the night when the heat of the day had faded.

"It ain't right, Brody." Tate pushed his hat back in that way he did when he was nervous. His knuckles were covered in grime. "We gotta put these back."

The smell of dynamite still lingered in the air, bitter and acrid. A cloud of dust, lit by the full desert moon, hovered by the hole in the cliff—the entrance to the mine we'd spent the last few months working. Our last blasting had spilled rubble across the threshold and amongst the stones were three skulls. Each one revealed the truth of its owner's demise; each one with the same neat bullet hole bored through the forehead.

Cold curled around us. I shrugged away a cloaking sense of dread.

"There's gold in there. I can smell it," I said.

And I could. I was the son of a miner, born to read the land, hear the song of quartz and the discordant twang of gold that sometimes runs through it. "There's somethin' big here. We just gotta dig a little deeper."

Tate bit his lip. He shifted and the lines of his face caught the shadows. "I got a bad feeling. This place is cursed."

The three skulls lay on the ground at our feet. Their grins seemed indifferent to me.

And what did Tate understand anyhow? He was the son of a gunslinger, no miner's blood in him. He was built big and broad, good help on a shovel and a pick, but he knew nothing about rock, about cutting away layers of pale quartz to find its golden veins. I sure as hell didn't put any stock in his opinion on curses.

"You best leave the thinkin' to me, Tate."

Tate sighed, clearly not at ease. He stood and gathered up the skulls. "You keep on diggin' then.

I'm gonna go bury these somewhere else. You know, outta respect."

"Those folk are long past caring about respect. Just leave them by the creek."

Tate turned one of the skulls over. A glint of gold flashed in the empty cavity.

I leaned forward. "What's that?"

"Dunno." Tate shook the head over my hand. A nugget of gold, the size of my fist, fell into my palm.

I blinked, hardly daring to believe what I was seeing. A coyote's grin grew on my lips. "I told you I could smell it. This is what we came for!"

But my friend stepped back as if stung by a wasp. "Brody, put it back. We should bury these folk and get outta here."

Superstition and ignorance. "After months of digging? We ain't goin' nowhere, Tate."

"Disturbin' burial grounds is bad. I've heard stories."

"Didn't peg you as bein' afraid of ghosts. Well, you go bury them heads but I ain't giving up this gold."

"I'll make you…"

Not taking kindly to being told what to do, I grew real still.

Tate stood hunched, like he was trying to make

himself smaller as to not antagonise me, to try and make me see sense.

I reached for my pistol.

Tate frowned and stretched out his hand. "Don't you dare, Brody!"

The memory of Tate's eyes, white-ringed and wide, flashes before me. In my mind, his hand remains outstretched.

But at the time I'd *known* it was him or the gold.

Him or the gold.

If only gold could temper guilt like water did thirst.

But as once before and then again,
Bone will always shear and crack.
Blood will spill
And tattoo across hallowed sand.

Murderer.

Wild eyed, I swing left, my revolver suddenly in hand. Only now do I realise the grip is sticky with half-dried blood. The gun tumbles from my grip, thudding to the ground. I wipe my palm down my shirt, but the blood remains.

I blink and suck in a deep tremulous breath.

I don't want to remember.

But I do—

I remember how I held the gold in one hand and my gun in the other.

And I remember how Tate had looked, standing by the creek.

Desert gods
With crowns of cactus and stone
They wield dry lightning.
To resurrect the just dead.

Perhaps it is greed that turns a man to darkness. Perhaps this is the sum of my truth. I'd never killed a man before. I don't even know what drove me to do so in that moment. Tate hadn't done anything wrong. But his blood had been so very, very red, running from the bullet hole I put in his forehead. My stomach had soured with the sudden silence and the shame that followed the crack of that single gunshot. I hadn't known that blood would spray so far, or that the sand would absorb it so quickly.

But the skulls knew. They'd leered at me, their own bullet wounds violent, black marks against their yellowed bone. Their blank eye sockets had accused.

And as I'd stood over Tate's corpse, his features blurred by night and blood, I saw the curse in his dead eyes—those empty blue eyes, flecked black— pinned to the distant stars. I'd taken the shovel and dug a hole to hide my crime. When deep enough, and dark enough at that line where the gritty earth grew damp, I'd rolled him in. I laid the skulls on his chest and packed the dirt tightly over them all.

Then I'd taken the gold and ran.

For in these wildest places
Weird holds true.
Celestials are the jury
And the dread executioners.

Ahead, a line of knife-edged cliffs veers away to the left. The towering, bare stone faces are banded in lines of yellow and ochre red. At their base, a shadow beckons. A cave. The coolness is an oasis I can't deny. A few hours rest is what I need. A small respite to wait for the cooler hours of night. I turn towards the shelter.

The cave is shallow but offers ample cover. Its floor is soft, unmarked sand, powdery grains that have eroded away from the roof overhead. I drop to the ground with a heavy sigh and close my eyes. An almost-cool breeze smelling of clean earth curls around me. For a moment the memories fade.

Exhaustion weighs like chains across my shoulders. I drift, dreaming uncanny visions of blue skies, blood-red water, and the deep song of a landscape both ancient and wise.

I fall into the welcome oblivion.

It's the press of cold steel to my forehead that wakens me.

"I warned you," whispers a cracked and broken voice.

I jerk upright. The darkness outside is proof that I've slept through the afternoon. A silhouette looms over me, barring the exit. The gun pressed to my head is very real.

"I…I'm just a traveller," I say. "I'm lost out here."

"You're a murderer."

My shoulders clench. "Tate? Is that you?"

His shape is unmistakable. Tate shifts and the moonlight catches the lines of his face. He still carries the bullet wound, a shameful mark against his brow.

"Yes. No. Not alive. Not quite dead." Tate reaches over with his empty hand and rattles the skulls that hang from his belt. He has woven rope through their eye sockets to carry them. "Three murdered men. Killed long ago over the same gold you now carry. On my behalf they called to something in the desert, something old and deep, and it answered."

Tate touches the wound in his head, the purple bruising around it as dark as a thunderstorm on the horizon. "Like lightning it woke me. It helped me find you."

I swallow. The pressure of the gun's barrel against my head remains steady.

"I'm sorry. I'm so sorry. I don't know why I shot you."

Tate's chin tilts. "That gold was buried in the head of a murdered man. I told you it was cursed. I warned you."

"But I'm a miner. I was born to dig, born to find gold. How can I make this right?"

Tate glances down at the skulls. Their grins no longer seem indifferent. His bloodshot, blue eyes snap back to mine.

"Here." I fumble with the bag at my belt. I hold it out. "Take the gold, take it back. Please."

Tate grows still. His silence weighs like bedrock against bones.

My outstretched hand trembles. "Don't you dare, Tate!"

The hammer of the pistol at my head clicks, and I close my eyes.

Of course. Of course, I die here.

Because Tate never cared about the gold.

Tate was the son of a gunslinger.

THIS DARK ARCHITECT

Present Day

Guilt cripples a man when the chance to make things right is stolen. The 'what if' and the 'I should have' conversations circle, revealing, in stark relief, the limitations of my character. I find solace in the work I do, but abduction to this alien world has stripped me of all former arrogance. I take comfort only in the company given me; comfort in the knowledge that I am not alone in this place.

My cellmate, Adelaide, has been here far longer than I. She is a woman of striking features and a fierce disposition, but her incarceration weighs heavy. There is a hollow weariness to her that reminds me, in no small way, of my wife and of the last time I saw her.

My wife...my family...

Adelaide shuffles past me. As stubborn as she is, I know better than to voice any concern over her obvious discomfort. I overlook the stiffness to her gait and the state of her hands; the way her paint-stained knuckles are swollen, crooked by the demands of her work. I ignore her eyes, too, and the brightness in them that suggests an imminent descent into madness.

We both walk that same terrible line.

Adelaide pauses and peers over my shoulder. Already I anticipate her commentary. Unlike my own, her preferences typically lean toward the surrealist.

"You really think gothic styling is the way to go?" Adelaide's North Queensland accent reminds me of cobalt skies and red earth—of the outback she says she hails from.

I tip my chin toward the window. "Teras says the Athana are expecting to crown a new Vassilissa in the coming years. This temple will be hers. Maintaining the existing aesthetic is safest."

Adelaide glances outside at the mustard-yellow, desert landscape. A line of distant sand dunes ripple in the midday heat. They shudder behind the heavy-set, yet graceful dwellings our captors inhabit—buildings that most closely resemble the gothic architecture of old-world Earth.

"Teras is just trying to frighten you."

"That's not true. He's always treated us kindly."

Adelaide shrugs. "Still, we are prisoners and you're an architect. Use your imagination. Play a bit and screw with their minds."

It's tempting.

"What would you suggest?" I straighten the plans and carefully detailed elevations. My hand-inked linework is elegant. Even though I'm held captive and forced to work on this project, I find joy in creation—in sketch design and documentation. I've always loved drawing buildings, loved imagining spaces in three dimensions and communicating them in two.

"Change the viewing lines," says Adelaide, her brow wrinkled as she considers the layouts. "Skew the Euclidian geometry."

I smile. "Surrealism may not need engineering to stand, but a building does."

"Form follows function, right?"

"True."

"Well, make the form screw with their minds. That's the function."

I take my ruler in hand and Adelaide smiles. I'm

glad I can give her reason to do so. Some adjustments can be made. A skewed perspective will stand and be subtle poison to the psyche. My pencil scratches across the paper. When our captors inhabit the final built space, they'll sense something off-kilter, but not identify the source.

"What will you work on today?" I ask.

Her head turns toward the huge oil painting sitting by the barred window. A riot of colour swirls across the canvas, indigo and green, lines of melted trees with gold-hued roots buried in a scarlet ocean —Adelaide's own philosophy of beauty skewed.

"An easy day ahead. The foyer piece is finished. I've messed with them too, though they don't know it. I painted a scene from home."

My heart clenches and I bite my lip.

It's been months since I last saw home.

———

Six Months Ago

"Duncan." My wife Lorena's tone accuses. "You promised you wouldn't go again so soon. You only just got home."

I pause in the doorway, laptop bag clutched in one hand, my back turned. I don't want to look at her. I'd rather be anywhere else but here.

"I'll be back in a week."

"But…"

I swivel, eyes narrowed. "I have to go to work."

Lorena, in her wrinkled cardigan, no make-up and hair pulled into a messy bun, steps back. I wonder what she sees in my face that inspires the desire to retreat. Does she suspect the truth? I frown, watching her twist her hands around each other. She looks so threadbare, nothing like the dark-eyed, svelte lawyer I married.

Motherhood has not been kind to her.

I have not been kind to her.

My treacherous conscience bites as our daughter, Bea, starts crying from the other room. The indignant wail of a two-month-old wanting to be fed. Lorena glances at the door leading to the bedroom.

"Please just wait for a minute, and I'll settle her," she says. "Let's talk before you go."

Lorena hurries out of the room.

A part of me knows I should stay, the part of me that once loved her.

But it is too late for that. There's no way back to where we were.

I quietly close the door as I leave.

Present Day

The twin suns have set for the day, replaced by night and the feeble light of a distant moon. The breeze coming in from the window still carries the lingering heat of this place, a heat that soaks into your bones. My mind circles, restless. Thoughts of my wife and daughter haunt me, swollen with the sting of regret.

Time has gifted me perspective. I wish I had waited and spoken with Lorena that day. Deep down, I still loved her and should have tried harder. Given the chance I'd do things differently now. I'd be a better man.

Footsteps resonate in the hall outside. The slither of soft robes whispers over the sandstone. Sweat prickles across my skin. This sound is our calendar. Has it been seven nights already? I resist the urge to rise, instead swallowing the sudden, sour taste in my mouth.

The lock rattles and the door cracks open. Adelaide, her bedroll set out against the wall opposite mine, whimpers. I hadn't realised she was awake, but perhaps she'd kept better track of the days than I and knew what was coming. The silent being who visits us in the dead of every seventh night never reveals her face. I only know that she is the Vassilissa, the Athana's alien queen, and the dark architect of our existence. She is also shrewd, careful to spread the load of her requirements on our bodies equally. She never takes enough to kill, but she also never, ever stops taking.

And tonight, it's Adelaide's turn, just as it was my own at the last visitation.

The Vassilissa slips into the room, her dark, cowled outline drawn out against the shadows. Adelaide scrambles upright, her back pressed against the wall. The whites of her eyes catch against the night like eclipsed moons, wide with fear.

I hate that I am powerless to help her.

Adelaide screams.

I turn to face the wall, eyes squeezed tightly shut.

Adelaide has bandaged her throat in a clean but paint-stained cloth. She moves stiffly around the studio, her features ragged and grey in the early morning light. Last night's ordeal has her looking even more so like parchment, fragile and threadbare.

I avoid making eye contact with her. I know all too well the shame that comes with the dawn.

Adelaide sits carefully at the table and takes a bite of the coarse flatbread I toasted for her. She chews slowly—painfully.

"Are you okay?" I ask.

"I'm exhausted."

"But are you okay?"

She nods, only a shadow of movement. "No skin taken this time."

I frown. The Vassilissa both drinks our blood and harvests of our skin. There is no rhythm to what she takes, and no explanation offered as to why. There is only ever the pain.

Pain better not dwelt upon.

"Why don't you come with me this morning?" I ask. "I need to take some more measurements to finalise the site plan."

Adelaide swallows her mouthful with a wince. Her grey eyes catch mine.

"How do you keep going, Duncan? I am all but done."

"I just don't accept that there's an alternative."

Her fingers worry at the bandage around her throat. "You know we'll never leave here."

I touch the scars on my own neck and feel the stretch of older scabs tracking across my shoulders. I recoil from the memory of an ice-cold blade slicing away sheets of fragile skin, the sensation of the Vassilissa's reptilian tongue lapping at my wounds. The thick saliva she leaves behind seals the lesions but does nothing for the lingering trauma.

Adelaide returns the flatbread to her plate. "She'll keep harvesting from us until we are nothing but scar tissue. Then she'll have us buried, nameless, in that desert out there."

I circle the table and place my hands on her brittle shoulders. "Please don't give up."

Adelaide sighs, the sound heavy with sorrow and regret. "I am stretched thin, Duncan. There isn't much of me left."

"Just stick with me a little while longer."

"What's the point?"

I lean in close. "There must be a way out of here."

Adelaide closes her eyes. "You're a dreamer."

"I just don't want to let *her* win."

"Doesn't mean you aren't a dreamer too." Adelaide's voice lowers. "I've been working at the bars in the window. Help me get them out and we can end this. The drop down is at least fifty meters. We can jump together. It'll be quick."

Lorena. Bea. I've already let them down so much...

"I'm not a quitter and neither are you."

A familiar rattle and the studio door swings

open. Adelaide straightens. I step back from her as the alien we have come to know best, Teras, enters. Tall and lithe, he looks almost human, except for the smattering of black and gold scales across his pallid brow.

I catch his gaze and shake my head. He frowns at my unspoken warning and his amber gaze shifts to Adelaide. Specks of blood have seeped through the fabric of her bandage. Teras's lips press thin. Still silent, he approaches her, and Adelaide lets him gently unwind the wrappings at her neck. The wound is worse than I imagined, with deep purple bruising circling two long tears half scabbed over, half weeping blood.

An annoyed huff of air hisses out of Teras's nose.

"I am sorry she left you like this," he whispers. Teras licks his index finger and presses his saliva to the weeping sores. The blood coagulates and he carefully winds the bandage back into place.

Adelaide looks away. "Thank you," she mutters.

"Yes. Thanks," I say, hoping this small kindness will help Adelaide endure for another day.

Eager to shift focus, I gesture to the table. "Please sit, Teras. I've finished the new façade drawings for you."

Our minder, who usually spends his mornings with us discussing the new temple on behalf of the

Vassilissa, shakes his head. Tension holds his features tight.

"Is everything all right?" I ask.

Teras's lips twitch. "I've been ordered…" His chin lifts. "The temple design must be completed by the next eclipse." The words are spoken just slightly too fast, a hint of something dark lingering behind his tone.

"I'm almost done," I say. "We just need those final measurements."

Teras nods. "I'll organise a guard to take you now."

"Can Adelaide come too? She could do with a change of scenery."

Teras glances again at the bandage on my friend's neck. "Not today. She is required elsewhere."

"Elsewhere?" I ask.

The alien's hands clench. "Her work on the temple decor is complete. The Vassilissa wishes Adelaide to be brought to her."

"*She* visited her last night," I growl.

"She wishes to see her again."

Adelaide presses a hand to her mouth. I imagine she's thinking of the window and her plan to avoid whatever comes next.

I step in front of her. "I need help to finalise detailing for the facade. Tell your queen that."

"Duncan. I'm sorry."

"At least try!"

Teras sighs. He reaches for Adelaide and gently gathers up her wrist. She struggles and his grip tightens. He tugs at the shoulder of her shirt.

"Don't!" she snarls.

Her sleeve slips. I gasp as Adelaide looks away, her breaths quick and angry.

Even living in such close quarters, she has always been careful to maintain her privacy when dressing. But I should've guessed. Her skin is scarred from neck to wrist. My own breaths quicken.

She wrenches away, fleeing Teras's grip. Her gaze, dark and tormented, catches mine.

"Don't you dare pity me, Duncan."

"Not pity," I reply. "Never that for you."

"Listen." Teras blinks and his voice lowers. "I have orders but no intention to follow them."

"You won't?" I ask.

"The situation beyond these walls is changing," whispers Teras. "The Vassilissa is preparing to fight the Indigenous inhabitants, the Anguis. They want us to leave their planet. That's why she fed so heavily on you last night, Adelaide. Human blood gives her far greater strength than the Anguis blood we typically drink."

Teras frowns. "But the Anguis are right; we don't

belong here, and I tire of the queen's cruelty. I want no part in what's coming, and so I aim to free you."

"Free? How?" asks Adelaide, tone as flat and hard as sun-baked rock. "There's no way out of this hellhole."

"There are places to hide in the desert. It's dangerous to get out of the city and a difficult journey to follow, but it can be done." Teras glances at me. "Duncan, you must keep the guards busy with those measurements at the temple site so I can smuggle her out."

I consider Adelaide's physical frailty. "I'm not sure she'll survive hard travel."

"She must try, or die here today."

"You can't take me too?" I hate how my voice cracks on the words.

Teras's face softens. "I will come back for you. Right now, the Vassilissa still needs you to finish the temple for her successor, so you are safe. With the Anguis amassing in the desert, though, she is being pushed to sacrifice Adelaide. She wants something only our female friend here can give her."

I almost don't want to know. "What is that?"

"Adelaide's identity—her face."

"My face?" Adelaide's eyes slew left to catch mine. "Why my face?"

Teras's haunted gaze lowers. "Because the Anguis

know what the Vassilissa looks like, and she needs a disguise."

"She wants to wear my face?"

"The Anguis are sympathetic to humans. If they breach the city and find you here, they will protect you. The Vassilissa is hoping that in looking like you, she will remain safe."

"I'll cut my own face off before I let that bitch have it," snarls Adelaide.

"Let's hope it won't come to that," whispers Teras.

Six Months Ago

Winter grips the Australian countryside, the skies hunkering grey and low. I press the heater on in the car and the warmth radiates out of the vents and across my chilled hands. My phone buzzes and Lorena's number flashes up on the screen. I tap 'end', sending her to voicemail.

I have nothing to say to her, not yet. I'm not willing to part with the secret I've kept these last months. I want to savour this feeling of being alive, a life untainted by the tears that my wife will inevitably cry. Because ever since I was contracted to work for the Australian Space Agency's lunar housing project, I've enjoyed the game—the clandestine meetings in busy offices.

I smile at the memory of white-blonde hair running through my fingers, ruby lips, and the smell of jasmine on sun-kissed skin. I know it isn't love I feel, but selfish animal attraction. But Elodie, vibrant and authoritative, Director of Operations at the Australian Space Agency, is everything my wife once was, but no longer is. She is a perfect distraction.

Present Day

A small satchel is packed with water and food. I finish by pushing in the single thin blanket I own.

"Don't." Adelaide rests her hand on my wrist. "You might need that."

I shake my head. "I'll be happier knowing you have it."

Adelaide wraps her arms around me and buries her head in my shoulder.

"This isn't goodbye," she whispers.

I squeeze her gently, focusing on her warmth and the scent of oil paint lingering in her hair.

"Make sure you get out," I say, "and I'll see you soon."

"We have to go," says Teras, shouldering the small satchel.

Adelaide steps out of the circle of my arms.

"Soon."

"Yes. Soon," I reply, hoping it is the truth.

Teras reaches the door as a new sound floats in through the window. Thin cries, carried on a scrap of heated breeze. Teras turns, brows lowered. The pitched noise rises.

"What's that?" asks Adelaide.

"Anguis battle cries." Teras bites his bottom lip.

I rush to the window. In the distance, the sands buckle, dunes surging into dense breakers, edges frothed by wind-caught particles. The waves swell impossibly until they burst, crashing and slithering into slips streaked in ebony and gold. The Anguis erupt from the sand in an undulating tide of muscled legs, sleek golden heads, and black-scaled bodies. The sand-eating lizards look to be over six meters in length, their razored teeth gleaming like polished iron in the daylight.

Terrifying.

Beautiful.

"The attack has begun!" Teras swivels away from the window. "The streets will be chaos. Maybe I *can* get you both out at the same time."

"How?" asks Adelaide, her words bleeding scepticism.

Teras grins, wild and alien. "If we can get you to the Anguis in the city, they will take you both away from this place."

Adelaide frowns. "And if they kill you before we can explain?"

Teras's grin widens even further. "Then I'll die having done the right thing."

"Why risk yourself for us?" I ask.

Teras's smile fades. "Because I remember what it means to be human."

My eyebrows rise. "Human?"

Shouts sound from the corridor outside our rooms. Running footsteps pass our door.

"Human. Vampire. Outcast. In the last three thousand years, we Athana have been all these things."

"All of you?" asks Adelaide.

"Yes."

Six Months Ago

.   .   .

I taste peppermint tea as Elodie presses her mouth hard against mine. She moans as I brush her throat with my fingertips. Then she breaks the kiss and leans back, her hair sliding like water across my hand.

"Are you familiar with 16th-century European architecture?" she whispers.

"What?" I pause, my mouth held an inch away from hers.

Elodie gently pulls further away from me.

"We need to talk about this right now?" I ask.

Elodie's grin intoxicates.

I bite my lip and lean back. "What do you want to know?"

"Just if you know much about it?"

"I did my honours thesis on the subject."

"I love that about you." Every bit the compelling seductress, she tips her shoulder forward. "I had some thoughts on including some of that old-world aesthetic into your lunar design proposals."

I kiss her gently behind her ear. "I can design anything you want."

She laughs. "Good, and it'll be a perfect excuse to spend more time with me."

Somewhere deep inside, a small part of me—the

part that still perhaps loves Lorena—screams in warning.

End whatever this is. Now. Before you lose everything.

Present Day

The vaulted corridor outside our cell is empty but the air is pregnant with expectation. The door to a guardroom stands ajar at the far end. I glance in as Teras leads us inside. The room is empty except for a table holding three empty cups and a deck of scattered cards. Teras snatches two cloaks from the hooks adjacent to the door and hands them to me. I swing one over Adelaide, careful to mind her injury. I shrug the second cloak over myself, wrinkling my nose at the previous owner's almost reptile-like stench.

"This is never going to work," whispers Adelaide.

"Keep it on," says Teras. "We need to ward off casual observation. If the guards see you, they'll kill you on sight."

We cling close together as we hurry, faces hidden in the folds of our pungent disguise. But perhaps the smell is also a boon. I lower my chin as several armed Athana shove past us, hurrying to the upper levels. I hold my breath as we press against the walls to let them pass, and while they should have been able to scent us, they do not.

Adelaide pulls her cloak tighter.

"We'll head for the lower gate," says Teras.

I nod. "Lead the way."

***

Six Months Ago

Lorena suspects. She approached me this morning in that rational manner that defines her.

"Are you seeing someone else?"

I shrugged. "Should you go back to work, so you have real problems to think about?"

The twinge of guilt I'd felt at my words was proof enough that I was being cruel.

Her brow had puckered, and her gaze then slid to the floor. She'd nodded once and left the room.

No outbursts, none of the tears I had expected. Just grace. That deep, inherent grace she's always had and of which I had forgotten.

For a moment, I found her beautiful again.

I *almost* called out after her but then convinced myself otherwise.

Grace is not passion, and I am a man starved for the latter.

I lift my chin, focusing instead on what is to come. Elodie. She feeds what I need, and she is waiting for me.

The road to her house is long and winding. Old-growth forest lines the verge, the canopy hiding the sun and holding emerald shadows close. Outside, sweeping vistas briefly catch my eye from between the trees—distant green rolling hills and yellow pastures, fences lined in green, all beneath the brilliant blue of a clear Queensland sky.

I flick the radio on. Music fills the car and I tap the steering wheel to its beat. The song skips as the digital radio signal drops in and out. I sing the lost words in between.

The radio suddenly crackles, screeching static pouring throughout the car. I wince and tap the radio button off.

"Damn signal."

The car's proximity alert beeps and it self-brakes. I lurch against the seatbelt, chest clenched against the unexpected motion.

"Damn it!"

Then I glance up. What looks to be a sleek, high-tech plane hovers just above the road ahead. Some kind of fancy RAAF warplane?

There are no bases near here...

Present Day

The Anguis have taken over the streets. Teras keeps us to the shadows between the buildings as battle cries filter around us, the Athana and the Anguis both fighting and dying. We turn a corner to find a bitter skirmish raging ahead, foes locked together in a rising cloud of dust and the scent of alien blood.

"This way," directs Teras, leading us down a smaller alleyway.

I glance at Adelaide. She is hunched low in the cloak, but her steps are steady.

The path opens onto an empty, sunlit courtyard. Across the way stands a towering structure, one of many in the city that are reminiscent of Gothic cathedrals. The yellow stone blocks gleam almost gold in the light, and the grand, arched entry beckons.

Teras swings to face us, his eyes shadowed. "This is a vacant priestess's dwelling. There's a bunker beneath. We can hide there until the conflict has calmed and then we'll find an Anguis. Move fast and quiet."

We sprint across the courtyard, footsteps muffled by the sand. When Adelaide stumbles, I catch her around the waist and keep us moving.

Inside the building is quiet; a lofty space, sparsely furnished. Rugs and low couches are placed artfully, each a place for rest, reflection, or prayer. A sandstone altar, stained with dark-green, clotted Anguis blood, holds the centre. High up on the walls are murals painted in gilt, blue, and scarlet—a range of scenes. Humans gathered behind fences. Spaceships. Skulls and goblets filled with scarlet. Anguis strung up from their necks, blood streaming down their distended sides.

Somehow it feels as if those paintings are alive.

I don't realise I've stopped until Teras pushes me forward.

"Our history," he says.

He hastens to the altar and kneels. A concealed lever clicks and a stone plate in the floor yaws open. A staircase leads down.

We crowd in and close the hatch. The darkness is absolute; only the air, warm and close, offers comfort. A spark ignites, growing to become a flame. Teras shoulders past us, holding a lit torch.

"Follow me."

The stair opens out at the bottom, flaring as it meets a smooth flagstone floor. Teras lifts the torch higher to reveal a drawing room of sorts. Lush rugs sprawl across the floor, more low couches upholstered in maroon velveteen and walls lined with shelves holding a library's worth of books bound in green and brown leathers.

Treasures pilfered from Earth, just as we were?

I pause as a baby's cry fills the room.

I pivot, searching for the source of the terrible sound.

Terrible, because it's a cry I absolutely recognise.

Six Months Ago

I only remember the warplane. I don't know how I was brought onboard but know for certain that the scale of the interior is off, the perspective somehow warped. I squint against the brilliant lights overhead and struggle against cold iron manacles that bind me to a hard, metal bed. I jerk my wrists up, trying to break the bonds, but only manage to break my skin. Blood drips down my fingers. Whispers fill the room behind me, voices like snakeskins whispering across paper.

"What am I doing here?" I snarl. "What do you want?"

More whispers. No answers.

Anger turns to fear. Sweat prickles across the back of my neck.

"Please let me go."

The whispers stop.

The lights go dark.

Gravity shifts; my perception skews.

And a sudden, overwhelming sense of momentum crushes me into the bed. I blink and try to breathe. I try to stay conscious.

But the laws of physics have other ideas.

Present Day

Teras crouches protectively in front of me, teeth bared. Adelaide braces herself against my back.

"It's *her*!" hisses Teras.

Adelaide stiffens.

A high-backed chair facing the library shelves turns and my gut lurches as I recognise the woman seated upon it.

Elodie? Impossible!

In contrast to her flowing black dress, my ex-lover's skin glows, clear and smooth as eggshell. Her eyes, hard as amber-coloured stone, take us in.

Elodie's brittle gaze then turns downward. The silken ends of her hair brush a small bundle held in her arms. The bundle shifts and cries out again.

"Your daughter is beautiful, Duncan," she says. "She looks just like her mother."

A sense of the surreal descends as reality tilts and my separate lives collide. I've been so focused on survival, so desperate to escape, to return home and fix everything that I broke, I've not even thought of Elodie since I arrived.

"How are you here? Why do you have Bea?" I ask.

Elodie straightens. "I am the Vassilissa," she says. "And Bea is here because she needs a mother."

Vassilissa? Mother?

The discordant thoughts plough together. Elodie smiles in that wicked way I know so well.

"I'll give your wife credit," she says, "she didn't let

her daughter go without a fight. More than can be said for her father."

"Where is Lorena?"

Elodie strokes Bea's small face. Her silence speaks volumes.

Lorena is dead.

The fragile hope I've been clinging to, of reconciliation—of redemption—falls away, replaced with hatred, regret, and sorrow—a tsunami of emotion condensing into one white-hot ember.

I can never make things right now.

Forgive me, Lorena.

My daughter's small fists wave in the air. My arms ache with the desire to snatch her. But cold logic holds me still. I take a deep breath and focus. I can still save Bea.

"Don't hurt her."

Elodie's lips curl down into a simper. "I've no intention of hurting her. Bea will be crowned as the new Vassilissa: the first since we were rendered outcast so long ago."

Human. Vampire. Outcast...

I need time. My mind races, considering options...

"At least let me say goodbye to my daughter."

"No."

"Why not?"

"You're without integrity, Duncan. You abandoned her. She's *mine* now."

My resolve cracks. "You seduced me."

"You let yourself be seduced."

"I've changed."

"No, you haven't." Elodie leans forward. "And you have no business claiming to be her father."

"Maybe not, but you aren't her mother either. You aren't even half the woman Lorena was."

Elodie's eyes thin. "I don't have to be, because Lorena's no longer a woman. She's a corpse."

My grief swallows any further words.

Elodie half turns, her conversation with me over. Her chin tilts as her regard falls upon Teras. She considers his position of defence as if it is of little concern.

"Teras," she says, voice as smooth as marble. "You have served me faithfully for centuries. Why do you stand against me now?"

"Because what you want is wrong, Vassilissa."

The lines around her mouth constrict. "I understand your conflict. It is not easy to stay the course. But you are Athana; your loyalty is to me. I will forgive you if you surrender Adelaide to me now. You know I need her."

Teras rises. "No, Vassilissa."

Elodie's face hardens, her disappointment clear

as she leans over and places Bea into a basket sitting by her chair.

She straightens. "As you wish."

I barely register the swiftness of movement as Elodie leaps, her black skirts billowing like storm clouds. She ploughs into Teras, our protector grunting as he is knocked across the room. He slides to halt against the far wall, limbs splayed and still. There's no time to tell if he is dead or just unconscious.

Elodie shoves past me with a snarl. Adelaide retreats a step, but her eyes blaze with challenge. Elodie laughs, lunges and grabs her. She pushes Adelaide to her knees and with a deep growl, bites down onto my friend's neck. Adelaide cries out, but the Vassilissa is too strong.

I roar as adrenaline fires me to action. With a shoulder lowered, I collide into Elodie. Her bite breaks with a wet tear, and she is thrown across the floor. Two metres away, the Vassilissa rises to a crouch and hisses at me, lips dripping scarlet.

"You stay the hell there!" I growl, low.

Elodie seems momentarily taken aback. I crawl to Adelaide. Her breaths are ragged as I pull her into my lap. I ignore the spreading warmth of her blood across my legs.

"I've got you," I say, trying to keep the tremor

from my voice. I press my palm to her throat, but the lacerated artery pumps more blood from between my fingers.

Adelaide coughs; her fingers reach for mine. "Save your daughter..."

Her hand falls.

Elodie giggles, sharp-edged as shattered glass. "Think of it this way, at least she's free."

I hold Adelaide closer. My whole being trembles. How could I have ever desired Elodie? Where Lorena had held grace behind her weariness, there is an ugliness behind the Vassilissa's beauty that I never recognised. Now, I want nothing more than to crush the life from her—to save Bea, to avenge Lorena, who fought for our daughter, and dear Adelaide who suffered so much for so long at this monster's hand.

Elodie wipes her sleeve across her scarlet-stained mouth and stands. She seems stronger. Adelaide's blood has invigorated her.

"Let me show you the truth," she says.

She reaches up behind her left ear and scratches down her neck. Her fingernails dig into the flesh, and she pulls. A slab of skin peels free from her face, a quiet ripping sound like the rind of an orange being torn away. I bite my tongue as alien features appear from behind the mask—a face half-human, half-reptilian.

Elodie clears away the last clinging threads of a clear, jelly-like slime left from behind the husk. A final tear at the neck and a larger slab pulls away from her shoulder also. Black and gold scales gleam there.

She drops the mask to the ground, her mouth screwed up in distaste. "They serve a purpose, but I do hate wearing human flesh suits."

Bile stings the back of my throat.

Elodie smirks. "I'm sorry. You liked that face, didn't you, Duncan?"

A swallow the cocktail of nausea and disgust coiling up my throat.

"I didn't know what was behind it." I try for calm, but anger resonates.

"And what is that?" says Elodie.

"A monster."

"Your ancestors made me a monster."

"No. I think you like being one."

Elodie leans forward, her teeth bared. "I had no choice! We Athana came from Earth, we the blood-drinkers—the once-immortals—cast adrift in our vessels, sent into the stars centuries ago. The ancients—the Atlanteans, the Greeks, and the Egyptians—they cast us out. We were forced to make a home here on this barren planet. And we were *so* hungry by then."

Something about the way she says "hungry" makes my skin crawl.

Human.

Vampire.

Outcast...

Monster.

Above us, faint sounds seep through the stone—the roars of those still fighting.

"We fed on the Anguis," continues Elodie. "Blood to sustain us but, blood that changed us. We were cursed, taking on their characteristics, becoming part-vampire, part-reptile. Our venom lost potency. That is why I took your daughter. I am...diminished. Long-lived but no longer immortal." She glances at Bea and a single word hangs unspoken.

Successor.

"But why *my* daughter?"

Elodie sniffs. "The night I chose your family, I saw you leave your office, deep in thought. Your creator's heart and obvious unhappiness were a perfect recipe. I knew I could control you, and like your friend, Adelaide, harness your creative skills to change the visual narrative of this planet. Art and architecture define dynasties. This planet will be my legacy."

Before I can reply, an explosion rocks the room. Thrown to the floor, I protect my head as the roof above collapses. My ears ring as dust and debris rain down. One sound is soon replaced by yet another—a high-pitched screech from Elodie. I glance at her. She's back by her chair—on the ground next to it—an arm held protectively over Bea's basket. My daughter, unseen within, wails. Elodie's teeth glitter as she rises, hair greyed with dust and her neck sheeted in green-red-streaked blood.

I roll to my knees. The room sways. Uncanny cries herald a wave of long, reptilian bodies that slither in through the hole in the ceiling. At least fifty Anguis. Elodie lowers deeper into a crouch, her white-knuckled hands held pressed to the floor.

As the lizards surge toward her, I know my daughter is also in their way.

I'm knocked down by the powerful hindquarters of an Anguis, racing past. I'm kicked again by another, biting my tongue and tasting the warm salt of blood. I roll, choking on the peppery scent of reptile that overpowers all. But any desire for self-preservation fades as my daughter wails louder. In that sound I hear the accusation toward a father who failed her, the grief for a mother she will never remember, and the hatred toward the vampiric Vassilissa that ruined us all.

I will make a difference—

I will be a better man.

I shove my way through the battling creatures. Great scaled flanks jostle around me, long iron-silver teeth flash, gnashing. Elodie flits between them all, supernaturally fast.

Somehow, I make it to Teras. His eyes flicker open as I shake him.

"Thank God!" I pull up my sleeve and jam my wrist against his mouth. "Drink!"

His lips are dry, and his teeth cut like knives through my skin. But by now, I am used to such pain. Teras's breaths grow hurried as he drinks, the grey pallor to his skin flushing suddenly with vitality. He pulls away, sobbing.

"Enough," he gasps. "That's enough." He pushes me aside, rises to his feet and enters the foray.

Hand clasped to my wounded wrist, I stand but stumble. I hold my balance for a moment but am spun about from behind by another Anguis. I trip and fall over a piece of masonry. Pain blossoms deep in my gut—the kind of deep ache that signals nothing good. I cry out and curl over my wound.

Senses blur as the pain continues to grow. I recognise Elodie's screech from somewhere between the jostling Anguis. The reptiles hiss in reply, rasping and sibilant. I close my eyes. Something heavy hits the floor and the room grows still.

The tenuous silence trembles. I open my eyes to

find the great lizards circling me. There, only metres away, lies Elodie with her throat torn out. Death has turned her skin to lined parchment, the years of her existence finally revealed.

Footsteps.

The Anguis part. Teras, his lips still red with my blood, approaches. In his arms rests a small bundle, its legs kicking, small hands clenched into fists. Bea's cry is a most welcome sound.

I sit up. The pain overwhelms. Teras kneels by my side. He gently places Bea in my arms. Her eyes are serious and as dark as night.

She does look like her mother.

"You saved her?" I bite my lip.

Teras nods. "Yes."

"You did a better job than I did."

"We did it together."

Around us, the Anguis turn away. They begin to climb the walls, taking their exit back through the ceiling. With Elodie dead, they seem calm now, resolved, and show no interest in hurting Teras.

Teras sits on the floor next to me and watches them go. "Strange. They must see me as an ally."

He runs a finger across Bea's tiny forehead and smiles. "I had a human daughter once," he says. "She was left behind on Earth when I was outcast." His bright eyes lift to meet mine. "I never saw her again, but her descendant…"

Teras looks at the ceiling. "I smelt the connection in the girl's blood the day they brought her here. An artist like Adelaide, and another I failed to save from the Vassilissa."

"She died?"

"Worse."

I glance at the ruin of the flesh mask Elodie threw so callously away, and a terrible thought manifests.

Teras seems to read my mind. "Yes. That."

The face I had desired.

Teras's own family had been harvested by the woman he served. I wonder if the Vassilissa knew or even cared.

The weight of so many sorrows is too heavy to bear. I draw a breath. I have always been selfish. I've only ever cared about myself, career recognition, and things of beauty. It hurts to know I could have been so much more, and yet, maybe it's not too late.

I gently kiss Bea.

"I love you," I whisper, my voice breaking on the words that I should have been saying to her since the day she was born.

My daughter sneezes.

I smile and kiss her once more. Then I gently

hand her over to Teras. "Be a better father to her than I was."

I clutch my stomach and smile without warmth.

Teras's features soften. He gathers Bea gently to his chest again. "I'll watch over her for you. She will be safe."

"I know." I swallow the warm blood gathering in the back of my throat. "And something else…"

"Anything."

"Lorena—she was a good woman. Make sure Bea knows what her mother sacrificed for her. And Adelaide. Bury her. Make sure her name is remembered."

Teras squeezes my shoulder. "I will. And for you too. I'll see your temple is built and that Adelaide's work fills the halls."

I nod, too weary for words. I try to focus on brighter things than my inevitable end. I imagine Bea grown on a world where the Athana and the Anguis live peacefully and dream of the life she will live. I see her walking vaulted halls lit by the light of twin suns.

Minutes turn to moments and I'm thankful that Teras waits with me; thankful that he keeps my daughter at my side. I listen to her small noises. They fill my senses.

I draw another pain-laced breath and look up.

Not long now.

My attention drifts. And as it does, I am consumed by a wash of surrealist colours swirling across canvas, and the recollection of a dark-eyed, svelte, lawyer I once loved, holding my hand.

And all around me stand buildings with their Euclidian geometry slightly skewed.

ACKNOWLEDGMENTS

My sincere thanks go to the various editors and publishers who worked with me on the previously published stories in this collection. Thanks also to Matt Tighe, Samantha Murray, Lauren Elise Daniels, Geneve Flynn, Jan-Andrew Henderson and Pauline Yates. You are all extraordinary people and exceptionally talented authors. Your support, wicked senses of humour, and friendship make this work not seem like work at all.

I would also like to acknowledge Wayne, our family friend to whom this book is dedicated, and his beautiful family. Their resilience in the face of recent adversity is nothing short of inspirational. My dedication is only a small gesture toward recognition of that, but it is given with love.

And most importantly, as always, my family. Darren, Piper, and Dakota. Thank you for being my world.

REFERENCES

'Tenebrous' first appeared in the anthology, *The Zookeeper's Tales of Interstellar Oddities*, CAT Press, March 2020

'Of Slaves and Lions' first appeared in the anthology, *Stories of Survival*, Deadset Press, August 2021

'Death Interrupted' first appeared in the anthology, *Body of Work*, Canberra Speculative Fiction Guild, September 2023

'Stokehold' first appeared in the anthology *SNAFU: Punked*, Cohesion Press, October 2023

ABOUT THE AUTHOR

Pamela Jeffs is an Australian speculative fiction author with a background in Interior Architecture and Design. She has published numerous short story collections and has 90+ short stories featured in various national and international publications. Pamela won the 2023 Aurealis Award for Best Horror Short Story and the 2024 Australasian Shadows Award for Best Short Fiction. In previous years she shortlisted for numerous other Aurealis Awards, Ditmar Awards and Australasian Shadow Awards.

This Dark Architect and Other Grim Tales is her seventh collection. To discover more books by Pamela Jeffs, visit and subscribe at:

- www.pamelajeffs.com
- Facebook: @pamelajeffsauthor
- Twitter: @Pamela_Jeffs
- Instagram: @pamela_jeffs
- Bluesky: @pamelajeffs.bsky.social